Praise for *VietMan*

"[An] absorbing, gritty military novel . . . [Lliteras] wins the
reader's admiration with his loyalty to and compassion for his
battle-mauled patients . . . [he] spins his first-person narrative
with laconic prose and acerbic wit . . . [an] accomplished novel."
—*Publishers Weekly*

"[*Viet Man*] is forcefully written, a nice mix of style and sub-
ject, and it has much to say about life and death and war and
peace . . . Fine war fiction from a writer who's been there."
—*Booklist*

Also by D.S. Lliteras

VIET MAN

A NOVEL

D.S. LLITERAS

RAINBOW RIDGE
BOOKS

Cover and interior design by Frame25 Productions
Cover photographs © STILLFX c/o Shutterstock.com and
Andrey_Kuzmin c/o Shutterstock.com

Published by:
Rainbow Ridge Books
140 Rainbow Ridge Road
Faber, Virginia 22938
www.rainbowridgebooks.com
434-361-1723

If you are unable to order this book from your local
bookseller, you may order directly from the distributor.

Square One Publishers, Inc.
115 Herricks Road
Garden City Park, NY 11040
Phone: (516) 535-2010
Fax: (516) 535-2014
Toll-free: 877-900-BOOK

Library of Congress Cataloging-in-Publication Data applied for.

ISBN 978-1-937907-32-7

10 9 8 7 6 5 4 3 2 1

Printed on acid-free recycled paper in Canada

Dedicated to David Willson

CONTENTS

The Pound Cake War

While preparing for a patrol, everybody scrambled toward the fresh issue of C-rat cases in order to scavenge the pound cake. These short green cans were easy weight in a backpack, and easy to open with a P-38. Pound cake was a bona fide delicacy in the bush, and damn well worth the scramble.

One

THE CREATURE

You know, when you're running away from a hornet's nest to save yourself, there's no time to ponder the meaning of life.

What a decadent madness it is to be introspective. What a beautiful curse it is to see mortality.

And what a madness it was when that mortality was challenged during those years Uncle Sam subtracted from my life. In fact, one of those years almost cost me that life, which started when I found myself standing in this place called Da Nang after stepping off an Okinawa plane filled with faceless characters like myself.

Yeah. I remember.

I lit a cigarette, feeling pretty froggy about myself. I was a Doc, a Navy Hospital Corpsman, a medical man who'd been attached to the U.S. Marine Corps for the last two years. And since I'd been with various artillery units all that time, I figured that's where I'd end up: running sick calls and cleaning earwax out of half-deaf marines who blew up the countryside with various brands of artillery.

I had it all figured out on the inhale of my cigarette, but my figures didn't add up on my exhale when I heard we were all going to the grunts.

"A combat corpsman's life expectancy is two weeks with the grunts," one of us said.

I was screwed.

I looked around, but I knew there was no one to complain to who mattered or cared. We were all in it—whatever in it was. We were all scared. We were all thinking about this thing called combat.

I concentrated on my cigarette as I studied an approaching jeep that first zigged then zagged recklessly in our direction. The brakes screeched when the vehicle stopped. Its passenger, with notable rate on his collar, stood up to address us as the driver cut the engine.

"I'm Chief Totti and I need five volunteers for First Recon."

Several somebodies chuckled as new smokes were lit. Then ragged cynical laughter erupted and enveloped us like a fog wrapping around a new kind of collective creature shifting its weight to one side with a corresponding dismay.

"Go on, Chief," a member of the collective creature taunted. "Those guys are crazy."

"What's crazy?" said the chief.

Another member of the creature sneered. "I ain't joinin' no Recons to get myself kilt."

"Maybe you're already kilt, son."

Although I didn't step forward, I didn't speak the creature's language either. "The First Recons—are they like . . . like the kind of outfit where . . . where you'd find John Wayne?"

"Something like that," said the chief. He had a smirk I trusted. The kind that didn't give a damn if you believed him or not; the kind that didn't care how you thought.

"I'll go," I said.

Nervous gibes and harmless jeers assaulted me.

The creature recoiled from my position as one of its members addressed me. "Joinin' that outfit is a death sentence, brother."

"Yeah. Well. If I'm going to go, I'd like to go like John Wayne." I hopped into the back of the jeep, after throwing my seabag on board, and felt as reckless as the jeep when it lurched forward and swerved away from the bewildered huddle of men awaiting a fate as unknown as mine.

I don't remember anything about the ride; the countryside left no impression on me.

I took a hard final drag from my smoke and flicked the smoldering butt into the road then leaned against my seabag, feeling satisfied.

I'd done something to change the course of my life and it felt good. Until that moment, I had responded to a set of orders and a stack of plane tickets; I had accumulated a pile of arrivals and departures; I had flowed in one direction then another without introspection or perspective. I had been here and I had been there until, finally, I was going somewhere I had volunteered to go to, even though I did not know where this somewhere was. But this somewhere was mine and I was going to it by choice and that felt real and good for a change.

○○○○

I had a split personality in Vietnam because of my being a U.S. Navy Hospital Corpsman attached to the U.S. Marine Corps, which transformed me into a Fleet Marine Force (FMF) combat corpsman. At heart, I was a bell-bottomed white hat with a syringe in one hand and a cup of coffee in the

other. At soul, I was a green-faced jarhead with a battle dressing in one hand and an M-16 in the other. I belonged because
I was a Doc who fought alongside some of the best fighting
men in the world. I didn't belong because I was a Doc who
didn't know a damn thing about military science. But I was
going to meet combat and learn how to shoot an M-16 and
discover how to follow the guy in front of me and succeed in
becoming a bona fide grunt.

○ ○ ○ ○

Anyway, I was feeling pretty good sitting in that jeep not
knowing that my perceptions about Vietnam were seriously
blurred and would remain that way for the rest of my life.

We drove past a formidable compound of buildings,
which were protected by a wire fence reinforced with barbed
wire. The fence also separated the compound's vast and dusty
parking lot from the road that we were traveling on.

"That's Freedom Hill over there," said the chief. "That's
where you'll find the Exchange and the USO, as well as a
movie house and a place to eat that's not a chow hall."

I studied my surroundings as we zoomed along U.S. 1
toward the First Reconnaissance Battalion compound called
Camp Reasoner. All the military buildings on this road to
my Shangri-la were wood-framed, vented with screens on
all sides, painted green, and roofed with corrugated tin; all
the civilian structures looked worn out. Everything appeared
remarkably the same: military vehicles and men, Vietnamese
people and terrain.

When we reached the battalion area, we stopped in front
of the Battalion Aid Station. The chief hopped off the jeep
and wished me luck as he tucked my orders and my service

jacket, my medical records and my pay records under his left arm. Before I could ask him anything, he waved the driver on. The jeep lurched forward when the driver released the clutch.

"Where are we going?" I asked the driver.

"Alpha Company. Your new home. Their hooches are right over there." The jeep veered toward the row of hooches that he indicated. He skidded to a halt near a cement pathway, cut off the engine, and climbed out. "Come on."

I scrambled out of the jeep, slung my seabag over my shoulder, and followed the driver to the last hooch of the Alpha Company area.

I stepped into the dark hooch where several guys with no faces glanced at me with indifference. One of them found the energy to point at an empty rack, indicating it was mine. As soon as I parked my seabag beside it, the driver took me to supply, where I was issued my 782 gear, which consisted of a backpack, a web belt and suspenders, canteens and ammo pouches, a poncho and poncho liner, a gas mask, an entrenching tool, and a K-bar. Then I was led to the armory where I was issued an M-16 and enough magazines to fill up four ammo pouches.

The driver drove me back to my hooch and waited for me to parallel park this gear by my seabag. Then he took me to another supply building where I was issued camouflaged utilities and shorts, green tee shirts and socks, bush boots and a bush cover.

"What about skivvies?" I asked.

"Nobody wears skivvies here."

"Really?"

"Crotch-rot."

"I see."

Before I could do an about-face, I had a new home and an old rack; I had a rifle that felt like a toy and 782 gear that looked like Army surplus; I had an uncertain future and an unimportant past.

With a simple right-face, I met two hooch-mates who had arrived in-country three days earlier. They were destined to become close friends, as well as distant memories on a black wall—a memorial not yet constructed. Inside an hour, we were standing outside First Recon's enlisted club drinking beer and smoking pot and talking trash as I kept shifting my gaze from a familiar sky to an unfamiliar panorama of rice paddies and back.

I lit a cigarette and felt pretty smug on my inhale: life looked good from where I was standing. Life looked good.

◇◇◇◇

In a few days, I learned how to shoot my M-16, was shown how to put together my 782 gear, and was instructed on what kind of food to take and how much water to carry. They were in a hurry to get me into the bush since corpsmen were supposedly in short supply. And yet, I saw too many corpsmen occupying the Battalion Aid Station. Many of these guys had maneuvered themselves into a cushy rear echelon job after one or two patrols—something wasn't right.

Still, I had it better than the regular grunts who lived like dogs in the bush. Those guys never got a break from the monotony and the discomfort, the danger and the filth. It worked on a guy's head.

In Recon, however, our time in the bush was finite. We'd go out on a four- to ten-day patrol, depending on the mission, the weather, and the combat events while we were out there. When we were done or hurt, we'd saddle up, move to a designated LZ, get ourselves extracted from the war and back into a relatively safe and clean and sane environment for two or three days. After a few months, however, this dynamic also worked on a guy's head: War. Safety. War. Cleanliness. War. Hot meals in a chow hall. War. Beer parties and, well, you get the idea. This was a life of absolute extremes.

This is not a complaint. Merely an observation. The truth is: I was lucky, and luck is relative. The truth is: I am certain, in retrospect, that I would have died if I'd been sent to the grunts. It had not taken me long to realize how special this unit was and how good fate had been to me. You see, many of these guys operating in the Recon teams really wanted to be in this war. They were warriors; they didn't want an office-pogue's job. In fact, a lot of these guys had two and three extensions in-country and were proud of it.

I was entirely out of my league. But I was glad to be one of them. In fact, I became one of those guys who never went to a rear echelon billet. I wanted to stay with real men fighting in a real war; I wanted to be tough and fearless in order to fit in and be—even if it meant not being anymore.

But what twenty-year-old man believes in his not being anymore? And what twenty-year-old man worth his weight thinks there's a future beyond twenty-one?

My status in the hooch suddenly shifted one night after I returned from the club with plenty of beer and marijuana in me to soften my restraint and challenge those faceless guys head-on after a week of listening to their veteran bullshit about how great a bush corpsman the guy was that I had replaced. I stood before them and said that I was nothing like the doc I'd replaced and that I didn't give a damn how kick-ass he was in the bush. I said, they had me now—and they heard me.

I said, it was me now, damn it—and they liked me. They saw that I had a set of nuts and that I might have enough screws missing in my head to be what it takes to be there in a place that threatened all being. From that point on, my life became one long series of episodes. And from that point on, I was one of the boys; I was swallowed up by a creature that did not step away from me this time even though I did not know its language yet. And yet, I was accepted—somehow the creature seemed to know that I would always carry my weight, would always buy a round of beers, and would always share whatever brand of hardship that would burden the creature. This might seem like I knew something, but I didn't.

For instance, I never heard of friendly fire until I got to Vietnam. I didn't know such a thing existed until we were on a ridge line somewhere in the North. I didn't know where exactly; I simply followed the primary radioman in the same way that the M-79 man followed me.

Life was okay, even though I was on a patrol in the middle of nowhere hoping for a cigarette break when I heard a 105 artillery battery cut loose with two distinct barrages some-where in the infinite distance.

I thought: those poor VC bastards. They were toast.

I thought: I'm sure glad those 105s were our guys.

Then the world exploded and numerous trees came crashing down all around the frightened and paralyzed crea-ture of which I was a part—a creature that expressed itself in the form of Loopie, our primary radioman, screaming into the hand set, "Check fire! Check fire! Check fire!"—until the firing stopped.

When it was over, the dazed and bruised creature checked itself to see if it was seriously hurt. Miraculously, there were no injuries.

Then I heard the 105 battery cut loose again and I thought: Oh my God. We're meat.

We stood there. We cowered. The creature was at one with itself. The creature knew that death was going to rain from the sky.

The explosions blew me off my feet. More trees fell. More screams assaulted the indifferent universe.

"Check fire, check fire, check fire, God damn it, check fire!" Loopie shouted from the center of the frightened creature.

The first set of explosions crushed me into the present and made me a repentant beggar. The second set of explosions separated me from the creature and transformed me into a six-year-old boy praying for his life.

I thought: that's all it took to lose control of myself? That's all it took to separate me from myself?

A holy silence descended upon us. I stopped praying. Loopie stopped shouting. The creature started breathing again, but it remained wary over a craziness that always lurked around the corners of every patrol operating in God-knows-where-Indochina, on missions that always sounded like search and destroy—a term that did not reflect the uncertainty and the mistakes that were made while on missions with a creature that was supposed to be swift, silent, and deadly. But tell that to the NVA when they discovered our whereabouts the following day.

This new condition startled me like a cold bucket of water drenching my face and paralyzing my mind when our patrol leader ordered us to halt, then commanded us to pitch grenades at our enemy.

Until that moment, grenades were those bulky round pieces of death that added weight to my life. Until that moment, they were a fashion statement carried on my web belt like my gas mask that hung from the left side of my waist and my claymore mine that hung off my right side.

My patrol leader shouted. "Pitch those grenades, damn you, pitch them!"

"Grenade!" I heard myself scream. Its steel body was in my right hand and its pulled pin was hanging from the left forefinger of my mind. I had death prepared by this separation in my hand and I wasn't sure what to do with it.

I looked to my right then to my left. The other guys were pitching grenades into the surrounding jungle like mad cavemen throwing rocks. They made it look easy. It seemed so easy!

I stepped back with my right foot and extended my right arm behind me. I should have wriggled out of my backpack before death had me by the hand.

I hurled the grenade. But the grenade did not hurl. It went a short distance and, in fact, no distance at all. No! Death had landed too close to the creature.

I was terrified. I wanted to jump into the nearest depression for cover and abandon the creature. But I couldn't. For the love of God, I couldn't.

"Grenade!" I yelled. "Everybody down! Grenade!"

I wasn't going take for cover until I saw that everybody else had.

I was going to die. I was going to die!

I hit the ground as soon as I saw the last man roll out of harm's way. The explosion ripped into my mind: My God, please, don't kill anybody. Please!

"Is anybody hit?" the patrol leader shouted. "Is anybody hit?" He stood up. He reached over his left shoulder with his right hand. "I'm hit!" He tossed off his backpack. "Doc, I'm hit!"

I ran to his side, filled with guilt and fear, as the war continued around us.

A tiny piece of shrapnel had penetrated deeply into his shoulder. It wasn't serious, but it was going to take surgery to remove it. He would live to see more war.

But surgery could never remove the horror of that moment when I almost killed the creature and when I refused life until the creature was safe after one minor wound and after one minor test of courage or allegiance or something gastrointestinal.

Two

PREPARING FOR PATROL

Casey was one of the good guys who possessed the right blend of self-interest and generosity, honesty and humor, conformity and rebellion to give him charm and elicit my trust. He was a big character with coarse brown hair chopped into a crew cut, a good ol' boy from Missouri with a regional drawl as long as his heart and as genuine as his smile. His country-boy demeanor caused Easterners to underestimate his intelligence.

Performance in the bush was the great separator. Those who could stoically hack it were considered real bush marines. Numbers never lie. You either earned twenty or thirty patrols or you didn't. Performance never betrayed. You either endured the demands of the bush or you fell from grace.

Casey was brilliant in the bush. And I was more afraid of disgrace than I was of being killed or wounded.

I was lucky to know Casey. He was the guy who taught me what to take on a patrol and how to carry what I took. He was a seasoned veteran and a respectable opportunist who figured if he took care of his doc, his doc would take care of him.

After a team was scheduled for a patrol, two cases of C-rations and several cases of long-rations were issued. The

eight men involved would cannibalize these cases according
to individual tastes, as well as collective consideration. For
example, nobody packed more than one pound cake from the
C-rations since there were only two pound cakes per twelve-
meal case. Since half of us were definitely going into the bush
pound-cakeless, the competitive scramble to scavenge one of
these lightweight delicacies had to remain friendly and con-
siderate and, ultimately, unimportant.

I had some understanding of C-rations before arriving in
Vietnam, since field training was a fact of life for all stateside
marines and corpsmen. However, it was Casey who familiarized me entirely with long-rats, which were hermetically
sealed plastic packages of dehydrated food accompanied by
cigarettes and sugar, powdered cocoa and toilet paper, and a
variety of other supplemental items. Chicken and rice, beef
and rice, and spaghetti would become my favorite dehydrated
meals, which I managed to cannibalize without difficulty
because the other meals seemed to satisfy my comrades' tastes
for meat and potatoes or beans. I've never been a finicky eater,
however, and to have been denied a favorite meal would not
have been a great discomfort or disappointment to me.

Like I said, Casey familiarized me with the proper
arrangement of my 782 combat gear, with the adequate selec-
tion of my food, and with the proper method of loading my
magazines with M-16 rounds. His straightforward instructions, based on experience, brought me into focus; he forged
together the disassociated knowledge that all marines and
combat corpsmen possess after passing through basic and
advance training.

Casey reached into an opened C-rat case from underneath a nearby cot, pulled out an accessory pack, ripped open
the brown plastic bag, and poured its contents onto the cot: a

plastic spoon; a small packet of salt, pepper, and sugar; instant coffee, and non-dairy creamer; a tiny box of Chiclets and a small box containing four Chesterfield cigarettes; a green book of moisture-resistant matches and a tightly rolled wad of toilet paper held together by a beige paper wrapper. "There's also stuff like this in the long-rat packets that you can snag."

"Right."

"You don't want to take those large cans of C's—you know, meatballs and beans and such. Carry your weight in ammo and water. Stock up on light dehydrated long-rats and the stuff that comes out of these accessory packs like the powdered cocoa and sugar. Pillage the C-rats for pound cake and peanut butter, crackers and cheese spread, chocolate candy and stuff like that. I'll show you."

After loading my backpack with a random variety of brown long-rat packages, with an array of green C-rat cans, and with a half dozen packs of cigarettes, a camouflaged poncho liner, extra magazines of M-16 ammo, two more canteens of water, and two I.V. bottles of saline solution, I stepped back and peered at the swollen backpack. "Damn."

"Don't worry." Casey attached my rappelling rope onto the left side of my backpack by a D-ring. "You're gonna be a professional in no time."

"Just like you, right?"

Casey chuckled. "You ain't right, Doc."

"What."

"Well. Truth is, I'm just a redneck. I don't know nothin'."

"I don't believe that."

Casey grinned.

I cinched both top-straps of my backpack. "I don't' know."

"What."

"Me. A professional. That's scary."

"Can't help you there. That's the way things are around here." Casey took a deep breath then exhaled dramatically. "And just think: you and me are in a good place compared to those regular grunts out there."

"Yeah."

Casey attached a set of canvas suspenders to my web belt. "That's enough thinkin'. Too much of that will get you in trouble around here." He glanced at the remaining pile of 782 gear on the deck. "Let's have those magazine pouches and canteens."

Casey helped me attach several canteen and magazine pouches onto my web belt in a configuration that started from my left side and circled completely around my waist.

By the morning of my first patrol, my belt harness would be loaded in the following manner: a full M-16 magazine pouch with a fragmentation grenade snapped onto both sides of the pouch by small canvas straps, another full magazine pouch with two grenades, a third magazine pouch, four canteens, and a white phosphorous grenade. A red smoke canister would be attached vertically to my left suspender and a K-bar would be secured to my right suspender.

According to Casey, if things really got hot and running from the enemy became a desperate part of our defense, I could drop my backpack and lighten my load without losing my ammo and water.

I glanced at my Unit One medical bag, which I was very familiar with because of my training at the Marine Corps Base, Field Medical Service School in Camp Lejeune, North Carolina. This bag, which I would always carry on patrols, contained the tools of my trade: battle dressings and bandages, aspirin and morphine, roller gauze and adhesive tape, two small dark bottles of serum albumin, a bottle of Merthiolate, a surgical instrument kit, and a variety of other medical equipment.

"But I wouldn't advise dropping your medical bag."

"I'd never do that."

"Yeah, well, there's a lot of stuff in that bag, and weight has a habit of gettin' in the way when things get tough out there."

"Look here. I'll drop my Unit One when you drop your radio."

"That will never happen. I'm a regular RTO. I'm used to haulin' that extra twenty-three and a half pounds on my back along with that backup battery."

"And I'm a regular corpsman."

Casey grinned. "Yeah. I reckon so."

I studied my newly constructed 782 gear again. "Brother, we're mules."

"That's for sure."

I shook my head. "I don't see the glory, do you?"

"Shee-iit."

I lit a cigarette. "What brought you here?"

Casey grunted. "The law. And a woman." He lit a cigarette. "I was bored and broke. Harassed and between jobs." He took a thoughtful drag from his cigarette, held the smoke inside of him until he seemed to reach a conclusion then exhaled. "Besides. Uncle Sam needed me and . . . and, well, I reckon I needed the change in scenery." He smirked. "Hell, somebody's got to kick ass for his country."

"Right."

"Besides, I wasn't goin' into that damn no-good Army. I figured that to be a sure way of gettin' myself killed." Casey reached into an open case of long-rats that was underneath the rack beside us and picked out the chili con carne with beans. He ripped open the outer green packaging and poured the contents onto the nearby rack. An array of small packets, which supported the main meal, were strewn beside the brown hermetically sealed, freeze-dried chili con carne food packet: sugar, coffee, cream substitute, powdered cocoa, a coconut bar, toilet paper, and a white plastic spoon wrapped in a cellophane bag. "That coconut bar ain't for shit." He picked up the cream substitute, the powdered cocoa, and the sugar packet. "But this here, you want to carry as many of these in your top pocket as you can so you can get at them during a fifteen-minute break." He handed the packets to me. "Those all-day humps in the bush can be hard and this here stuff packs a nice energy kick."

I glanced at the packets. "What do I do with this stuff?"

Casey snatched the packets from me. "I'll show you." He ripped open the top of the cocoa packet and spread its opening to form a receptacle. Then he opened the sugar and cream substitute packets and poured them into the cocoa. "This ain't as goofy as it looks."

"I'm not saying anything."

Casey took a thoughtful drag from his cigarette. "You're goin' to make it. I've got a feelin' about you."

"If you say so."

Casey unsnapped a canteen cover from one of the 782 harnesses that hung from a rafter by its right suspender; it was hooked to a large nail. He pulled out a dark-green plastic canteen, unscrewed the cap, and trickled about a tablespoonful of water into the cocoa packet. "Hand me that spoon." He screwed the cap back on to the canteen and placed it on the window shelf while I pushed the handle of the spoon through the cellophane.

I pulled the spoon out of the bag. "Here you go."

Casey stuck the spoon into the cocoa packet, stirred the contents into a wet chocolate paste then handed me the receptacle. "That's the recipe."

I lifted the plastic spoon out of the packet and studied the thick dark paste.

"I know it don't look good, and it probably don't taste good right now. But in the bush it's ambrosia: wet, sweet, and chocolate. You'll see."

I crushed out my cigarette into a nearby ashtray on the window shelf, then stuck the spoon into my mouth. The concoction was sweet and gritty. "It tastes pretty good right now."

Casey nodded. "Like I said, you're goin' to make it."

"If eating this stuff is all it takes, I'm going to like it here."

"Yeah." Casey chuckled. "You've got the right amount of crazy in you."

I continued eating the chocolate paste. "So. You said something to me about the law. You know, back in the world. The law, you said. What was that about?"

"I'm just a common redneck, Doc."

"I don't believe that."

"A bar fight over a woman and a pool game is what did it to me." He lit another cigarette from what was left of his smoldering butt. "Stupid. Damn stupid." He crushed out the butt into an ashtray. "But I reckon trouble was always comin'."

"On account of what?"

"On account of," he grinned. "I'm a hellion, Doc. And hell is where all the interestin' people are, don't you think?"

"I hope so." I dropped the remainder of the cocoa packet into a trash can then lit a cigarette. "How did that bar fight turn out?"

"I'm here, ain't I?"

"Meaning what?"

"Meanin', that fella went to the hospital, I went to jail, and that woman walked out on both of us." He took a deep drag from his cigarette then exhaled slowly. He studied the smoke as if the smoke contained a hidden message. "That son of a bitch didn't know that I knew. When I walked in and saw my gal at the bar and him at the pool table—I knew." He nodded for emphasis. "You should've seen their fright. Yeah. When they saw me, they acted like they didn't know each other." His left eye twitched. "I played dumb. I eased over to the pool table and placed my quarter down to challenge the winner of the game." Casey's eyes grew ugly. "I knew he'd win that game. He couldn't help himself. He had to face me head on. He had to get close to the rattler." He chuckled. "Then I slid over to the bar beside my girl to wait my turn and ordered a beer. 'I thought you were workin' late, honey,' she said. 'Yeah, well, I'm not,' I said. She squirmed. She didn't know what to do. She glanced at that son of a bitch, as I reached for my beer, thinkin' that I wasn't watchin'." Casey looked at me as I took an attentive drag from my cigarette. "But I caught it all from the corner of my right eye. He was fuckin' her and she was fuckin' me. The bitch." He took a hard drag. "I should've hurt her as much as I hurt him but, hell, I made him pay for both of them."

"What did you do?"

"I waited for him to win then I eased over to the table and chalked up the loser's cue. 'It's you and me, partner,' I said. 'Rack 'em up,' he said, thinkin' he had me figured for a dumb ass. Oh, but I played him. I waited until he was nice and relaxed and home free before I ran the balls on the table down to the eight ball. Then I chalked up my cue, leaned over the table for my last shot, looked straight into his eyes and said, 'Is she good pussy?'" Casey shook his head. "The son of a bitch's eyes went wide. He knew he was caught. He knew he was dead meat. When he saw me catchin' him lookin' for an exit, he got cocky; it was a bluff I wasn't buyin', and he knew it. But he played it out anyway and I let him. I wanted him to sweat. I wanted him to understand that I was goin' to hurt him." Casey gritted his teeth. "The son of a bitch understood. And when he swung his cue stick, he missed me. The stick broke when it hit the edge of the pool table. Then I swung my stick, but I didn't miss." Casey grimaced. "I broke his arm good." Casey became lost in thought.

I took a drag from my cigarette. "Are you alright?"

Casey's expression grew darker. "I commenced to beatin' him to death. Damn. I couldn't stop myself. It took half the boys in that bar to pull me off of him." He blinked. "I went crazy." He took a drag from his cigarette. "I do that sometimes."

"Yeah. Well. You didn't kill him, did ya?"

"Nah. I almost killed him. Yeah. I messed him up pretty good. Women." Casey took a troubled drag from his cigarette. "That's what I get for drinkin' so much. I lost the pool game and my freedom and, well, a judge gave me a choice: the penitentiary or the Marine Corps."

I snickered. "So, that's what you meant by Uncle Sam needing you?"

Casey grinned. "I reckon. At first. But now, well, now—" Casey shook his head then grinned. "My country needs me. And there ain't no angels in hell, Doc."

"Good. I don't like angels."

"Right on, brother. Fuck a bunch of angels."

"Yeah. Fuck 'em." I studied my smoldering cigarette. "I'd like to think I'll do the right thing when it gets tough out there."

"Hell. You will."

"I don't know. I feel like I'm standing at a doorway about to step into something much bigger than myself."

"I'm goin' to give you some advice, and it ain't goin' to make any sense to you right now."

"Alright."

"Don't see. And if you do see, don't let it go inside of you. Whatever you do, well—that's between you and, and whatever it is you believe in." He crushed out his cigarette into the nearby ashtray. "I ain't very smart, but I'm a survivor."

"And I'm part of your surviving?"

"Yeah." Casey smiled. "I'm gonna take good care of you in the bush. You'll see. And you know what?"

"What?"

"You're goin' to keep us both from doin' the wrong thing."

"I don't know about that."

"That's alright. I know." Casey picked up the chili con carne package. "These long-rats aren't bad. They're easy to fix. Let me show ya." He ripped open the brown plastic bag and pulled out the freeze-dried main dish in the reconstitution package that had a white cardboard bottom to support the meal. "You unfold this clear bag and open it up like this." He poured water into the bag of food from the nearby canteen then used another white plastic spoon to stir the chili. "You'll never have hot water, so you need to let it soak for a while—especially for chili. Some of those beans in there never get soft. Still, they're better than C-rats." He folded the clear bag closed and set the spoon and the meal package on the window shelf. He lit a fresh cigarette from the remains of my smoldering butt that I was about to crush out. "The truth is, Doc, I was in love with that girl that walked out on me. Hell. She was no good. She was cheatin' on me all the time. It made me crazy. Crazy. I could've killed that fella. Hell, I was lucky I didn't. And for what? Women. They ain't no good. They can't be trusted. They can't." He crushed out my cigarette butt.

"That's not true and you know it."

"Maybe. But right now, I don't want to know the truth. Right now I'm here and she's fuckin' some other fella and, hell, nothin' makes any sense." He grabbed the chili package and opened it. "You got a girl waitin' for you back in the world?"

"No."

"Good."

"I . . . I had one."

"Oh. Well. You know how I feel about women." Casey picked up the white plastic spoon and stuck it into the chili con carne with beans. He gave the meal a final stir and presented the long-rat bag to me. "Taste it."

I accepted the bag, scooped out some of the chili, and ate it.

"What do you think?"

"Not bad. And I'm sure it'll taste better in the bush."

"That's right. Even water tastes sweet in the bush."

I took another bite. "Yeah. This is alright. It's good."

Casey slapped his thigh. "Damn, if you ain't a bona fide chow-hound."

I studied my fully loaded backpack, web belt harness, and Unit One medical bag. I was intimidated.

"Don't worry. You'll be able to hack the load."

"I hope so."

"Come on. Let's go to the club and have a beer. This is enough learnin' for one day."

"Yeah. I can use a beer."

Three

THE WARRIORS

I drank too much at the club and left Casey sitting with three opened cans of beer on a table crowded with beers and stories and dark laughter. I was drunk and tired and I wanted to get into my rack.

As I made my way across the Camp Reasoner compound toward Alpha Company, I suddenly felt that I belonged to First Recon and accepted my uncertain future with this unit.

When I arrived at my hooch, I avoided the guys when I entered. I laid down and closed my eyes. I almost felt content. My situation did not seem as bleak as on the morning of my arrival. I know: beer talk.

I was startled from my fragile repose when the door of my hooch was kicked open. I sat up on my rack.

The tall intruder remained outside near the door's threshold. He stood in the hooch-light that spilled into the darkness outside. "Your training is almost over, Doc. You'll be fragged for a patrol in a couple of days."

"Fragged. Okay." I stood up. I approached the imposing marine.

He kept the door open with his left boot.

I stepped outside. "That's—soon."

"We need docs." He let the door spring shut. He was blond and thin and shirtless. "I'm Corporal McDuggal. I'll be your assistant patrol leader."

"Where are we going?"

"You'll be briefed with the rest of us."

"Alright." I offered McDuggal a cigarette. "How long have you been in-country?"

McDuggal plucked a cigarette from my pack. "I'm on my third extension."

I lit his cigarette before lighting mine. "Damn. How long have you been here?"

He inhaled deeply then exhaled thoughtfully. "Since March of sixty-seven."

"Whoa. What are you trying to do, get yourself killed?"

"There's a war to fight."

"Right."

"And I'm here to fight it."

McDuggal and Casey were polar opposites of each other. Casey was a private first class who was ready to leave this country yesterday. Corporal McDuggal was of the warrior class who was determined to stay. Casey was a ground-pounding ex-grunt, a mud soldier, who did not seek glory. McDuggal was a pipelined trained recon, an elitist, who walked invincibly.

The difference between them could be seen in their eyes. McDuggal's were cold, Casey's were warm. McDuggal's eyes were calculating, distant. Casey's eyes were swirling, myopic. They represented one of the cultural opposites that existed in this unit. There were many: juicers versus heads, the junior enlisted against the lifers, short timers ignoring fresh meat, bush marines tolerating office-pogues, jarheads maligning squids, and, of course, blacks opposed to whites—yes, this was

the late sixties and civil rights unrest had infiltrated the ranks
of the green Marine Corps.

"Where are you from?" I asked.

"Boston." He started walking. "And you?"

I accompanied him. "Miami."

"Never been there."

"Yeah. Well. I've never been to Boston."

We stopped walking after we reached the opposite end of
Alpha Company.

McDuggal flipped his unfinished cigarette into the shadows where the orange glow bounced then rolled to a stand-
still. "I'm going to the club. You want a beer?"

"No thanks. I've had too many already."

"What's too many?"

I shrugged. "I don't know?"

McDuggal sauntered away from me because all that there
was between us had been said. The war had not bound us yet.
There were no patrols or deaths, no kills or regrets to share.

I turned around and headed back to my hooch. Light
spilled from the row of hooch windows on my right side and
lighted the shadowy sidewalk that ran the length of the Alpha
Company area. When I reached the last hooch, I heard the
door of the nearby latrine slam shut. A quiet figure emerged
from the shadows.

"Doc."

"Hey."

The guy stood before me prepared to remain silent; after
several days, he still hadn't spoken to me.

There was an intangible flatness to his demeanor, a
solemnity that attracted my curiosity. He behaved older than
his numerical age. His speech was measured, his movements
were economical, his expressions were never excessive. He

wore black-rimmed glasses above a set of tight lips and below a brown crew cut of hair. His dark eyes lacked luster, but not depth; his average height and weight left no impression.

I chuckled nervously. "You're . . . you're Mormon right?"

"That's what I'm called around here."

"You . . . you don't seem to like it much."

"Well. It's what is." He frowned. "I'm a member of the Church of Jesus Christ of Latter-Day Saints."

"Ahh. Yeah. I see. So . . . so that's why Mormon—"

"Always comes up. And it always sticks. I don't fight it anymore."

"Where are you from?"

"Utah."

"Of course. That's where the Mormon Church—"

"Of Jesus Christ of Latter-Day Saints—"

"Is located. Right. From Salt Lake City."

"Some of us."

"Yeah. Well. Miami. All of me."

Mormon's mouth twisted into an expression that almost passed for a grin. "I've been fragged for the same patrol that you're going on."

"Really? It's my first one."

"I know." Mormon's monotone did not reveal his attitude toward me.

"I just ran into McDuggal. He didn't tell me much about the patrol."

"There's nothing much to talk about until after the briefing."

"Right. That's what I got from him."

"He's a good man. He doesn't like bullshit."

"I got that. Loud and clear."

"If you need any help, let me know."

"Thanks. I can use all the help I can get. Casey's watching out for me too."

"You'll be alright."

"You think so?"

"As alright as any of us." Mormon walked passed me in a manner indicating that our conversation was over.

I watched him disappear into the gloom. "*Are* we alright?"

"As alright as God will allow."

Mormon's remark left me feeling uneasy. His baritone voice was devoid of reassurance.

As I approached my hooch, a redheaded, freckled-face guy dressed in a pair of camouflage shorts and jungle boots, a green tee shirt and a white sailor's hat stumbled outside. A smoldering joint in his mouth revealed the source of his disorientation. He recognized me immediately. "Hey, Doc!" He plucked the joint from his mouth and offered it to me."

"Thanks, Red." I took a hit and passed it back to him.

"So. You're a head. That's good."

"I'll try almost anything to get high."

"Way to go." Red adjusted his sailor's hat toward the back of his head.

"Where did you get that?"

"Off a sailor in Guantanamo Bay, Cuba. He snatched my cover from me at the EM Club. Man. It turned out to be one hell of a bar fight."

"Who came out ahead?"

"I got his squidly white hat, don't I?"

"Squids and jarheads usually stay away from each other in Gitmo, Cuba."

"The fleet was in and the guys at the marine barracks were—well, we were bored and I guess we needed to get into trouble."

"I spent four months in Gitmo. Mortar Battery, One-Ten."

"Shit. Then you know what I'm talking about." Red passed the joint back to me. "I'm your M-79 man on your first patrol."

I took a hard drag from the joint. "Hello, M-79 man."

The bite of the thick marijuana smoke made me cough. "That's. Good. Stuff." I continued to cough as I handed the joint back to him.

"It's the only good thing around here." He planted the joint in his mouth, adjusted the white sailor's hat over his forehead, and started walking toward a narrow pathway that ran between two hooches. "There's a party in one of the Delta Company hooches. There's sure to be plenty of opium and speed and . . . and whatever. You want to come?"

"Naw. I'll catch up with you later. Maybe."

"Alright." Red entered the dark pathway and headed for Delta Company. "We won't be hard to find if you change your mind. Delta Company hooches run parallel to Alpha Company—back to back."

"Thanks."

"Hoo-ya."

"Hoo-ya." I approached my hooch, opened the door, and entered its crowded interior.

The wooden walls and the two-by-four support beams were painted white, the floor and the overhead were raw plywood. There were two rows of canvas cots, which lined both sides of the hooch. These ten racks were orbited by an array of 782 gear and weapons from above, and surrounded by lockers and foot lockers and stereo speakers on the floor. The congested conditions were intensified by the glut of objects that occupied all the flat surfaces including the spaces underneath each cot. The long window shelves on both sides of the hooch, which ran the entire length of the structure below the hooch-length screened windows, were covered with a variety of things that served the needs of men destined to go back to war: cartons of cigarettes, beer cans and soft drinks, bottles of hot sauce, cans of WD-40, boxes of film, rolls of toilet paper; ditty bags, cleaning equipment, stray magazines; bush covers and articles of clothing, ashtrays and candles and candy bars.

The floor was cluttered with jungle boots and sandals, canvas gear and R&R suitcases, cannibalized boxes of C-rats and long-rats. The walls were decorated with Recon Unit plaques and photos of naked women, with pictures cut from magazines and thumb-tacked for display; even a pair of black Viet Cong pajamas, taken off a confirmed kill while on patrol, had been tacked to the interior of the hooch's front door along with an Asian conical hat made of bamboo. This strange scarecrow, with an NVA flag hanging above it, reminded us of our enemy's invincible presence, as well as with our enemy's mortal absence.

Most of the canvas cots were padded on top with camou-flaged poncho liners, but some of the cots were padded with a thin narrow mattress.

Aside from the occasional snapshot of a high school sweetheart thumb-tacked to the wall at the head of a cot, there was no display of sentiment in these surroundings. Sentiment revealed weakness, and weakness was a door not to be opened.

On the second cot to my right, Tennessee Bolton was lying on his back with his khaki shorts unbuttoned—he was masturbating proudly. "Hey, Doc! Watcha doin'?"

"Damn, Bolton, put that thing away. Aren't you embar-rassed?"

"Hell, no. I'm horny." He stroked his erect penis with increased affection. "I'm thinkin' about my R&R in Hong

Kong. Gee-zuuz-keey-rice." His eyes glazed over before clos-
ing them. "I bought two whores my first day and screwed
them both all night. Yeow! That was good pussy." Bolton
opened his eyes. "Then again, I never had any bad pussy." He
glanced at a broad and husky man with black hair, Sergeant
Dinky Dow, who was sitting on a corner cot in line with the
row of cots on the left side of the hooch. His small snubbed
features suited his round impish face. "Have you heard of any
bad pussy, Dinky Dow?"

"Naw. And Doc's right. Put that damn thing away."

"Come on, Sarge."

"Put it away or go out to the shit-house and finish it off."

Bolton pulled his shorts over his deflating erection.
"Shit." He sat up and swung his legs off the cot. "I need a
beer." He slipped into a pair of sandals, stood up, and buttoned his shorts.

"Don't trip on that thing on your way out."

"Ha, ha." Bolton shuffled toward the hooch's entrance, as
he put on a tee shirt, and pushed open the front door. "Maybe
one of them bar wenches will be willing to give it up tonight."

"Don't count on it," said Dinky Dow.

"Yeah, yeah." Bolton stepped out of the hooch and let the
spring-latch slam the door shut.

"Is he always that loony?" I asked.

"Always," said Dinky Dow. "He's our tail-end-charlie. A
good man in the bush. He'll cover your ass every time."

"I don't doubt it."

"I'm going to be your patrol leader. I heard Casey's taken
you under his wing."

"I think so. McDuggal also offered to help me."

"I saw that. He's a good man. You're going out with *the
best* on your first patrol. You're lucky." He glanced at two guys

smoking cigarettes and playing cards on two empty boxes of C-rats placed side by side, which converted them into a small table between two cots. "That Apache Indian over there is our point man. He's the best in the business."

I glanced at a dark brown man with a hard, sinewy physique. His prominent nose separated a pair of narrow piercing eyes set deeply above his high cheekbones and placed well below his straight black hair that draped across a high forehead.

"Hey, Doc. I'm Lima." He had an American Indian accent. "And this crazy black dude who's losing his money to me is Dogen, your primary radioman."

I looked at the huge and muscular black man. His wide nose separated a pair of deep black eyes that suited his large facial features and prominent jaw.

Dogen waved at me without taking his eyes off his cards. "Doc."

"Dogen." I smiled at him, then at Lima. I didn't feel invisible anymore.

Dinky Dow spoke as if he had read my mind. "Now that you've been fragged, you're no longer a phantom—or a load."

"Ah. Well. I want to carry my weight."

"The reports from training about you are favorable."

"They are? Damn. I hope I can do right by you all."

"Don't worry, you will." Dinky Dow lit a cigarette. "Any man who doesn't pretend to be anything more than he is, is alright by me." His exhaled smoke italicized his compliment.

"Well. I guess . . . I guess I'm whatever, well . . . whatever it is I am."

"I don't need a training report. I've been watching you."

"I haven't been here long."

"It don't take long." He took a hard drag from his cigarette. "You'll do."

I reached into my pocket for my pack of smokes and pulled out a cigarette. "I've been meaning to ask you: Dinky Dow?"

"Yeah. That's Vietnamese for crazy."

I planted the cigarette in my mouth and lit it with my Zippo lighter. "Are you?"

"You'll find out," Dogen interjected, his dark eyes focused relentlessly on his cards. "Dinky Dow on your first patrol to Elephant Valley. What a draw."

Lima punctuated Dogen's cold statement with a sinister chuckle.

I let the heavy exhale of my smoke serve as my response.

Four

TRAINING

The last day of training ended with a rappelling evolution from the belly of a hovering CH-46 Sea Knight. The only other time I'd ever rappelled was during the training evolution on the afternoon of the day before at a nearby mountainside.

The equipment used in this dangerous evolution was crude: a length of rope wrapped around the waist and looped under both thighs then hooked in the front with a metal D-ring.

When it was my turn in line to step near the edge of the opened trap door on the deck of the chopper, I clamped the D-ring onto the rappelling line as I peered through the square door and studied the open space between the hovering craft and the ground: the dynamic increase and decrease of the ground's distance was dramatic. The speed of the green light shuffle to the door, the urgency of the men snapping on their D-rings, and the intensity of jumping into the abyss in order to keep up with the man in front and stay ahead of the man behind, erased any possibility of hesitation:

I jumped.

The ground and the sky whirled around me while I descended on the rappelling line that wrapped behind me and rested against my back. My left arm extended upward, allowing my gloved hand to act as a stabilizer, while my right arm served as a speed monitor and brake depending on the extension of the arm and the grip of my right hand on the line: the right arm fully extended with a loose grip allowed me to slide downward; pulling my arm toward my chest with a firm grip acted as a brake to slow my rate of descent.

Reaching the end of the rappelling line during descent meant that the hovering chopper had been lifted higher from the ground by the elements than the pilot intended, which meant you were in for a long drop and a hard landing.

I was lucky: I made it to the ground with line to spare and plenty of time to get out from underneath the man above me.

Training was over. The patrol's briefing was tomorrow. Yesterday, I'd managed to learn what our missions were generally about: to conduct reconnaissance and surveillance operations within the patrol's assigned area of operation; to detect VC and NVA troop movement; to locate, monitor, and destroy enemy communications; to locate and destroy enemy base camps, supply routes, and supply caches; to conduct ambushes and captures; to search and destroy.

Last night the meaning of search and destroy occupied my imagination. And in a couple of days, well—there would be no distance between my notions of the foreseeable from my experiences of the really real. My slim accomplishments during my week of training made the beers taste better at the club each night, which is where I was—the club: a place to think about my past, a place to soften the harassing thoughts about my future.

I stood up and stared at my empty can of beer and I slipped my hands into my trouser pockets to support my fragile confidence.

Four days ago, I'd managed to shoot my M-16 on the firing range in the semi-automatic and automatic settings well enough to realize that I was going to be as dangerous as my enemy in the bush.

I walked back to my hooch to get some sleep.

Five

THE BRIEFING

The room was dominated by the erect posture of an intelligence officer and a large wall map.

I peered at the men seated with me at the long table; the same men I had become familiar with during my chaotic week of training evolutions. Each of their neutral facial expressions were as flat as a set of corresponding black and white photographs. This gallery of portraits squinted through an acidic curl of cigarette smoke and sat in a silence caused by premature cynicism. This assemblage of young men in their physical prime restrained themselves like high-strung thoroughbreds lined up at a race track's starting gate; they tolerated this air-conditioned-officer who flourished a wooden map pointer against a two-dimensional geographical abstraction that represented his entire depth of involvement in this dirty little war. These eight pairs of patient eyes rested upon this starched-uniformed-being who documented our patrol's composition and roster, authorized our special weapons and observation equipment, issued our operational maps, informed us of our insertion and extraction coordinates, revealed our call sign and radio frequencies, and stated our mission objectives.

I heard something about Elephant Valley and noted the circular motion of the wooden pointer emphasizing a section of the wall map. My attention drifted away from the map's contour lines and landmarks toward the members of this recon team preparing for a patrol:

Lima, our point man, was crazy and fearless. Dinky Dow, our patrol leader, was tough and competent. McDuggal, our assistant patrol leader, was aloof and intelligent. Dogen, our primary radio man, was solid and steady. Red, our M-79 man, was wild and strong. Casey, our back-up radioman, was easy going and dependable. Mormon, our rifleman, was quiet and inscrutable. Bolton, our tail-end-charlie, was edgy and dangerous. And I, the combat corpsman, was overwhelmed but determined.

Again, I heard something about Elephant Valley. About confirmed enemy kills. About captured documents.

I lit a cigarette and thought about how completely dependent on these men I was going to have to be—starting tomorrow. In the bush. Somewhere in Vietnam.

Six

THE LZ

Zero dark thirty in the morning: this meant long before day-break.

I did not check the time when I was roused out of my rack to saddle up and rendezvous outside before going to the landing zone. The orange glow of lit cigarettes that clustered actively near our weapons cleaning station reminded me of fireflies.

Upon us: silence prevailed, low-grade tension enveloped, anticipation tempered.

The unfamiliar bulk of my gear, along with the expectation of an increase in its weight after we arrived at the LZ, concerned me. The armorers would be waiting to hang ordnance onto our web belts and suspenders like lead ornaments upon Christmas trees: fragmentation and smoke grenades, white phosphorous and incendiary grenades, claymore mines and, perhaps, one of us would be issued a LAAW—a shoulder-fired, 66-millimeter disposable rocket launcher made of fiberglass.

"Let's go," said Dinky Dow. "We're burning daylight."

Nobody responded verbally. We followed him out of the company area and across the Camp Reasoner compound then descended the steep path to the asphalt LZ where numerous

teams were already staged in small groups on the north end of
the vast asphalt that felt vaster by the darkness. The light of
predawn created numerous silhouettes of steadfast men and
strewn gear.

Daylight blinked at us while we were still at the southern
end of the LZ, near the on-line armory shack located beside
the mouth of the narrow supply road. Sergeant Dinky Dow
monitored the two corporals, support marines assigned to
the armory, in order to insure that we were being issued the
desired ordnance. He also wanted to know who was getting
what. For example, grenades: all of us carried fragmentation,
but he wanted to know who was carrying a red or a green or
a yellow smoke, and who was carrying a white phosphorous
or an incendiary grenade. Knowing who had what ordnance
made it possible for him to direct an order at the right guy
after making enemy contact. Our array of grenades clung to
us like deadly birds perched on barren winter trees. Curiously,
the added weight increased my mental confidence rather than
my physical burden.

The professional behavior of these support marines reflected
their desire to provide us with safe and reliable ordinance.

After completing our load-out, we went to the north end
of the LZ and bivouacked among the other clusters of men.
Then we occupied ourselves by streaking our faces with the
color green and gray, using sticks of greasepaint.

Sunlight finally cracked over the horizon and illuminated
the sea of quiet men, of canvas gear, of inert weaponry—all,
waiting to go to war this morning.

The sky, our avenue to the unknown, was deep and
infinite. I heard Dinky Dow say that the ceiling was above
two thousand feet. I heard the distant sound of a couple of

CH-46 transports, a Huey gunship, and a Cobra. They were approaching us from the southeast.

Dust. Wind. Debris. Hurry up and wait.

The noise and wind of the incoming choppers invaded the LZ and stirred the recon teams. Men who were sprawled on the hard ground and propped up on their backpacks turned their attention toward these landing aircraft.

Nobody stood up even after the pilots shut down their engines. There was no reason to hurry up then wait: it could be another hour before a couple of teams were designated to embark on the parked CH-46 Sea Knights.

I lit a cigarette and inhaled the surrounding activity.

On the northeastern side of the LZ, there was a large supply of food and water and ammunition staged for transport to an OP. These high elevation observation posts were manned by twelve to sixteen marines and a half-dozen ARVNs for about thirty days.

The officer in charge of the LZ suddenly designated the team beside us to board the chopper.

Nobody got cute. There were no wisecracks or banal bon voyages—only a silence that honored their departure because this was the really real. They were going in.

I bit down on my cigarette filter.

"It won't be long for us now," said Casey.

I plucked the disfigured cigarette from my mouth. "How do you know?"

"Listen. More choppers are comin'. Once they get started, it's incomin' and outgoin' all mornin' long."

A few minutes after two teams boarded the transport choppers, the pilots started their engines: both Sea Knights, the Huey, and the Cobra.

Dust. Wind. Debris.

The noise of the choppers lifted to the sky and rushed away from us as two more CH-46s landed. The pilots waited for their outgoing teams to embark without shutting down their engines then swooped into the sky to make room for the other approaching choppers. I was surprised by the hurry-up portion of our wait when we were finally designated to go.

We approached the rear of the chopper and hustled inside of it through its lowered ramp. The first four men sat on the long canvas bench attached to the bulkhead on the left side and the last four men sat on the right side. Facing each other somehow increased the really real of our going to war.

Seven

A SMALL WAR

The flight. The insertion. The desertion of the choppers.

The unreality of lying on my belly next to seven other men on their bellies. The reality of a hostile environment threatening my existence.

The disbelief of no turning back, of no second chances, of no protection by those who love you.

The heat of the sun made the elephant grass seem taller and sharper. My disorientation made all points of a compass a geographical abstraction. I had no sense of direction. I had no idea which way we were going to go.

Sergeant Dinky Dow stood up and indicated, with a single wave of his left arm, that he wanted us to move out.

I got behind Dogen. Movement was a relief. Dogen's back was my focal point.

The increased thickness of the bush comforted me. I felt protected by the womb of heavy vegetation; its ability to conceal was as much to my advantage as it was to my enemy's.

I depended on the detachment of my mind, my physical stamina, and my trust for these men. I believed they knew where we were going and what we were doing and why we

were doing it. These men were my means of survival. My
mind drifted as I moved within the patrol's formation:

"Come on, Doc. We have time to go to a skivvy
house."

"A what?"

Casey's lustful grin broadened his face. "A
whorehouse, brother."

"Ahh."

"Come on. Dog Patch is just down the road
from here. We can thumb a ride and be there in
a few minutes."

I lit a cigarette. We were standing outside in
front of the Freedom Hill's Exchange complex on
a bright Vietnam day. Training had been canceled
for the afternoon, which left me free to hang out
with Casey who had seized the opportunity to take
me out of Camp Reasoner and show me around
Freedom Hill and the outskirts of Da Nang.

I exhaled the first of my smoke. "What's that
over there?"

"That's nothin'. The Red Cross. They ain't
nothin'."

"I thought they were here to help us."

"All talk and donuts."

"What's wrong with that?"

"Their talk ain't for the GI and their donuts
are stale. They don't give you nothin'."

I shrugged. "I don't want anything."

"Yeah. Well." Casey chuckled cynically. "The
thing is, they think they're better than you."

My attitude hardened. "Even here?"

"Go in there for yourself and find out."

"No. I believe you." I harassed my cigarette by repeatedly flicking the filter with the tip of my thumb. "Is there anything to that Freedom Hill restaurant over there?"

"Nah. The truth is, the only things that are good here are the cigarettes and the pogey-bait in the Exchange, and that movie house over there."

"A movie house." I turned toward the structure.

"Yeah, yeah."

"I wonder what's playing?"

"Forget that, Doc. Are you coming with me to the skivvy house or not?"

"Sure. Sure."

We crossed the parking lot, stood on the edge of U.S. 1, and hitched a ride on a truck heading toward the outskirts of Da Nang. Dog Patch is what we called our destination and, upon arrival, there was no question why this mean street intersection earned its name.

Dog Patch was the Vietnam version of an inner city slum. It was a main street crossroad with dilapidated structures that were constructed with inferior plywood and corrugated aluminum. Every structure looked as if it could be knocked down with a strong wind. Every structure needed paint and repair.

Military jeeps and trucks and armored vehicles, miniature three-wheeled buses and mopeds and unconventional vehicles glutted the Dog Patch streets. Pedestrians filled the spaces between the sad structures as well as on both sides of the congested dirt road: civilian women and children, merchants and Vietnamese soldiers, prostitutes and con men, and the ever-present American GI looking to gratify his personal vices—drugs and whores, gambling and black market trading, and God knows what else.

Casey and I were two ordinary marines traveling along the edge of this street looking for the kind of pleasures expected from men like us. We drew no attention because we were the common contributors to this upside-down, war-torn culture. Underneath this filth and chaos there was a quiet desperation prepared to erupt into violence.

"The mama-san that runs the place that we're going to is straight up and down. She won't rip you off."

A small Vietnamese woman, wearing a conical bamboo hat, walked past us with several cantankerous children orbiting around her.

"This way. Come on."

Casey did not notice the beautiful woman across the street, standing underneath a pink umbrella while waiting for a bus.

She was dressed in a pair of black silk pants and a white cotton blouse. A large white purse, made of fabric and painted with butterflies, hung from her right shoulder. Her arms were wrapped across her abdomen—her left arm above her right with her left hand holding up her pink umbrella.

I wanted to say hello, but our worlds were light years apart.

Her shoulder-length black hair was curled at the bottom.

"Hurry up, Doc. We're burning daylight."

I hustled alongside Casey. "So, you've been to this place before."

"Damn right. The mama-san there tries hard to look out for ya."

"What do you mean?"

"Skivvy houses are bad about rippin' ya off."

"Then why take a chance?"

"You're kiddin' me, right?"

"Well. It's kind of dumb. I mean, if you know they're going to steal from you and—"

"It don't mean nothin'. If you go into it with your eyes open, it don't mean nothin'. Besides, in a way, we're robbin' them as much as they're robbin' us."

"That doesn't sound right."

"What in hell is right? Besides, that thing between your legs has a mind of its own. You can't control that fierce hunger. Fierce. It's got to be fed."

"Well."

"Don't worry. That mama-san will look out for us. You'll see."

"I guess I will."

We walked past several small groups of soldiers surrounded by Vietnamese civilian men and women. Their body language suggested illegal business transactions. Corruption appeared to be the norm.

I paused momentarily and studied the squat conditions—the backdrop for military and civilian traffic, for legal and illegal commerce, for loitering and hustling pedestrians. War's poverty dominated this environment burdened by exhaust fumes and dust.

"What are you doin', Doc? Come on. This is the way."

"Okay, okay."

We approached a long row of corrugated-roofed structures in need of repair. They were miserable shanties without running water or electricity or window screens. Each hovel had a roof overhang supported by two-by-fours and scavenged poles; their doors had been reinforced and repaired so many times that they looked like wooden patchwork quilts.

Casey approached a young woman standing beside one of these doors. It had been propped open with a piece of broken cinder block—the entrance revealed a dark interior.

The black-haired beauty wore a western-style dress that was sleeveless and collarless and designed with pink horizontal pinstripes printed on a white fabric. The dress, which hugged her slender figure, tapered down to the tops of her knees. The wide black belt that was fastened around her narrow waist tightened the upper portion of her dress and accentuated her ample breasts.

As soon as Casey started speaking to her, an old woman stepped through the doorway's threshold and intercepted him. The sharp contrast between her and the young lady was startling.

The old woman was devoid of all western influences. She wore a bamboo conical hat, a white blouse, and a pair of pants as black as her teeth. Her pinched eyes burned with resolve and her lantern-jawed countenance demanded attention from those she addressed.

I didn't know if the mama-san recognized Casey or pretended to.

She moved like a spider. She ushered us inside the hovel.

The interior of the dwelling smelled like rotten fish and disinfectant. In the corner of the room, there was a young woman squatting by a turquoise plastic washtub. She glanced at us as she placed a white bar of soap on a nearby cinder block then grabbed a blouse floating in the tub and started scrubbing it against a washboard. There were several wet balls of clothing by her feet.

She was a beauty. Her long black hair was pulled back into a thick and shiny ponytail. As she scrubbed, the bottom of her white blouse rose above her black pajama pants and revealed her smooth, pale lower back.

Casey nudged me with his left elbow. "She's not a working girl."

But mama-san was perceptive and stepped toward me. "You want boom boom?" She pointed her thin forefinger at the washerwoman and began chattering in Vietnamese. The woman gazed at me then responded to the mama-san who nodded at her before nodding at me. "You boom boom, okay. Five MPC."

Casey grinned. "Damn, Doc. Looks like you already have a girlfriend."

She stood up and dried her hands on a nearby towel then approached me with a prefabricated smile.

"Five MPC," the mama-san repeated.

"Pay the old gal," said Casey.

I reached into my pocket for my small roll of cash, peeled off a five MPC bill, and gave it to the mama-san.

The mama-san addressed the washerwoman in Vietnamese again as she pulled Casey toward a door that led into another room.

"I'll meet you back here, little buddy. Mama-san has got someone in mind for me."

The mama-san tugged impatiently at his arm. "Five MPC. Come on. Five MPC."

As soon as Casey paid the old lady, she escorted him through the door into another room. The beautiful washerwoman touched my upper arm and encouraged me to follow her.

She led me into another stark interior. The cement floor was swept and the unpainted ply-wood walls were clean. At the center of the room, there was a wooden platform with a thin pallet on top. She guided me alongside of it then turned to me. I felt uneasy.

Her beautiful facial features were delicate, translucent, innocent—Vietnamese.

She took off her pants then raised her blouse above her breasts before she climbed onto the pallet. She laid on her back; her breasts were full, her nipples were dark. She spread her thin legs.

I was astonished. Scared. Hesitant.

She was equally astonished. Confused. Impatient.

She sat up. "You want boom boom?"

She smelled good.

She took me by the hand and encouraged me to join her.

As soon as I laid my rifle against the pallet, she unbuckled my belt, unbuttoned my pants, and pulled my pants down to the tops of my jungle boots. I felt ridiculous with my erection poking through the bottom of my camouflaged blouse. She pulled me to her as she laid back down.

Three children scampered into the room and giggled mischievously. I reached for my rifle, afraid they would try to steal it. She shouted at the kids until the mama-san stormed into the room and chased them out.

"Come," she said. "Boom boom. Quick."

Although the calmness of her voice unnerved me, I climbed onto the pallet. When I felt her hand grab my penis, I flinched then pulled away from her.

She was surprised. "You no want boom boom?"

I said, yes, but my body said, no.

She reached for me again, but I lost my erection along with my resolve. I didn't know what to do. I didn't want to be here: my fault, not Casey's.

I maneuvered off the pallet with difficulty because my pants were down to my ankles. I was embarrassed.

She sat up on the pallet and let her white blouse drop down to her waist. She glanced at my flaccid penis. "You very horny."

"Yes. I'm very horny." I pulled up my pants. "Sorry. Sorry." I buttoned my pants then buckled my belt.

"You come back?"

I glanced at her tender nakedness. "Yeah. I come back." I grabbed my rifle and smiled at her. "Thank you. I come back."

She had a perplexed expression etched across her exotic face.

I backed away from her, still mesmerized by her beauty. I stumbled over an ammo can filled with folded clothes. "Sorry."

I opened the door behind me and entered the other room. Several kids ran past me and went into the room that I had just left.

I wanted to get out of there.

I saw the turquoise plastic wash basin full of gray soapy water . . . then I saw the door. I dashed across the dark room, pushed open the door, and stepped outside.

The black-haired beauty in the western-style dress was no longer standing by the door under the shade of the tin veranda. I lit a cigarette. I decided that I would avoid places like this from now on. I took a hard drag. I was confused by my

physical desire and my feelings of uncleanliness. I
waited for Casey.

He finally stumbled out of the shanty blink-
ing at the sunlight. "Hey, Doc! How about that?"
He slapped my back. "I told you I'd take care of
ya, didn't I?"

"Yeah."

"Pretty good, huh?"

"Yeah."

Casey lit a cigarette then whispered dramatically. "Do you remember that pretty thing stan-
din' at the doorway there?"

"Ah . . . no."

"Well." He showed his teeth. "She's pretty
good." He slapped my back again. "Come on.
Let's get us a beer."

"That's a good idea."

"Stick with me partner, I've got plenty of
them." Casey stepped into the street and headed
toward the intersection. "Come on."

I followed him until . . .

. . . until to my surprise, I almost bumped into Dogen. I was
standing in Elephant Valley, not Dog Patch. I was following Dogen, not Casey. To make matters worse, I had been
unaware that a serious situation had developed. The team had
come to a stop. I glanced back at Casey in an effort to find out
what was going on. His weapon was at the ready. I glanced
ahead at Dogen. His weapon was at the ready.

I kept quiet.

I kept still.

I kept my head.

Then I saw Lima back away from where he had been and approach McDuggal and Dinky Dow.

Word was passed up the line: Lima smelled an ambush. We waited.

McDuggal, Lima, and Mormon were ordered to pitch grenades into the suspected area and Red was ordered to follow up with HE rounds from his M-79.

I watched Mormon. He knelt on the ground and laid his rifle down beside him. He unsnapped a grenade from one of his ammo pouches and straightened the pin. Then he held the smooth, sheet-metaled, olive-drab body of the grenade in his right hand and positioned himself in order to toss the grenade as accurately as possible at the targeted area. He waited until the others were at the ready before placing the tips of his fingers over the grenade's spoon and slipping his left index finger into the grenade's pull ring. He stood up. He waited.

Casualty producing hand grenades had a four- to five-second time delay and a killing radius of fifteen meters.

Mormon pulled his grenade pin as soon as he saw McDuggal and Lima pull theirs. Together, they released the safety levers, let the spoons fly, and tossed the grenades as hard as they could. Three explosions ripped into the bush.

Red shot an HE round into the same area. Another explosion. We waited.

We did not draw fire.

Lima clicked his rifle into semi-automatic and approached the target area.

We waited.

We had made enemy contact.

We had two confirmed kills: Viet Cong.

I was numb. Within hours of my first patrol, I was standing near two dead men. The one nearest me was young, lean,
smooth-faced. He wore a loose black shirt with his sleeves
rolled above his elbows and a pair of loose-fitting black shorts.
He had a single bandolier of ammo and an AK-47.

Sergeant Dinky Dow and Corporal McDuggal searched
the men. McDuggal reached into one of the dead man's pockets and found a beige pouch with a drawstring. He pulled
open the pouch and poured the contents on the ground: a
sewing kit, a brass belt buckle with a five-point star etched in
the center, a fishing hook joined to a lead sinker by a two-inch
nylon line, and a tiny bottle.

Where was God in this? I wondered.

I picked up the tiny bottle, unscrewed the green cap, and
sniffed: camphor. I studied the green label and read: Bai Lac.

I reached for a silent prayer.

Dark. Small-boned. High cheeks. Close-cropped black
hair. His Vietnamese facial features were tightly drawn with
an expression that challenged eternity.

McDuggal glanced at me. "Are you alright?"

"I'm fine."

"Don't get goofy on me."

"He's fine," said Dinky Dow. "Did you find anything else
on him besides that junk?"

"That's all he had," said McDuggal.

"Damn. This other one didn't have anything on him."

"They smell like fish." McDuggal stood up.

"Yeah. Well." Dinky Dow stood up. "Let's get out of here."

"Right."

As soon as Dinky Dow transmitted his short report to
Battalion Headquarters, Lima was leading us into the bush as
if nothing had happened.

Eight

A DISJOINTED WAR

The war's intensity increased with the accumulation of patrols that merged into a disjointed mental collage consisting of faces and places, enemy contacts and medevacs, airborne skies and strange landscapes.

Preparation for patrols after two or three days rest remained the same: Assigned a team. Attend a briefing. Prepare for the daybreak choppers at the LZ.

Stand-down from patrols after several days in the bush remained the same: The security of arriving at our LZ. The relief of returning unspent ordnance to the armorers. The welcome of the hooch's safety.

Emotional recovery from those killed or wounded in action remained the same: No guilt. No tears. No feelings other than emotional neutrality in this disjointed war.

∘∘∘∘

We were operating in a mountainous region when we made contact. Men were killed and wounded in action: three enemy KIAs, one WIA—Animal, our M-79 man.

There was no LZ for a medevac.

I applied an airtight pressure dressing over Animal's sucking chest wound. I spread a poncho liner over him. I injected him with morphine.

By the time I had him stabilized, I heard an incoming chopper responding to our call for a medevac.

Thank God.

The chopper found the break in the jungle's canopy and managed to lower a litter through it. I ran toward the litter and reached for it. But the rise and fall of the hovering chopper along with the pendulous swing of the litter prevented me from getting a hold of it.

Dirt kicked up near my feet.

I heard McDuggal holler. "Sniper!"

I had to get Animal out of here.

More dirt kicked up. There was an occasional ping. The litter remained painfully out of reach.

I was alone. Exposed. Trapped with the responsibility of caring for a wounded man.

I was going to die today. I was going to die. Everything lost color.

Noise muted. Movement slowed. Perceptions flattened.

I glanced behind me to see where the other guys were and caught Bolton's awed expression.

I grew calm, turned away from him, and looked up at the litter that continued swinging like a demented pendulum.

I grabbed the litter as soon as it swung within reach and brought it to Animal as quickly as the chopper could pay out the line. Bolton was waiting for me.

Dirt kicked up again as we strapped him into the litter.

We guided the litter as the chopper pulled it off the ground then we dashed for cover.

I flattened myself against the earth and listened to the sound of the chopper recede into the distance.

When I looked up, I saw green . . . green trees.

◦◦◦◦

After numerous patrols, the men became faceless, the days timeless, and the patrols numberless episodes in my life.

I can't remember how I discovered their intent to kill our six-week-old, boot-camp lieutenant, who had no business being our patrol leader. Stepping between the lieutenant's back and the muzzle of an M-16 made this an unforgettable episode.

I shook my head and I grimaced to emphasize my objection.

The tail-end-charlie and the back-up radioman frowned.

No, was my silent response to them.

I was bewildered by this kind of life-and-death situation. I was unable to allow such an act to occur.

We humped through the mountainous region and through the intense heat.

After two more attempts, I realized I had to do something other than display my disapproval. I decided to disrupt the patrol.

I swallowed my pride, feigned heat exhaustion, and collapsed before anyone was able to act upon their plan to kill our incompetent officer.

Casey hustled toward me, knelt down, and whispered, "What's wrong?"

I waved a feeble hand at him to display my helplessness. "Hot."

Within a few moments, the lieutenant approached Casey and whispered. "What's going on? What's happened?"

Caution prevented any of us from speaking above a whisper. Rudimentary hand signals, facial expressions, and body language provided emphasis and clarification. No matter how intense the confrontation, verbal communication was muted.

Casey glanced at me suspiciously, then answered the lieutenant. "I think it's heat exhaustion, Lieutenant."

"Heat ex—" the lieutenant hissed. He stepped away from me then muttered, "What a load."

The lieutenant's remark rankled me.

"Easy, little buddy," Casey murmured.

The lieutenant approached the assistant patrol leader to confer with him. His body language conveyed impatience and disgust.

Casey helped me out of my backpack and unbuckled my web belt. I sat up, hunched forward, and supported myself with my forearms against my thighs.

"Are you alright?"

"No. Yeah."

"We better go through the motions then."

"What," I muttered.

"You know what."

I grinned.

Casey shrugged. "You're a hard head." He unsnapped one of my canteen pouches and pulled out a canteen. He unscrewed the cap then handed me the canteen as he reached into his trouser pockets for a small bottle of salt tablets.

I drank some water. "That damn L-T."

"Don't pay him any attention," Casey whispered, as he handed me two salt tablets.

Tommy, our tail-end-charlie, approached us. "You should have let us waste him, Doc."

"No way."

"He's a dumb shit."

"Shhh, keep it down, Tommy." Casey stole a glance. "The lieutenant's lookin' this way."

I ignored Casey. "And what are we if . . . if . . . forget it, man. No way."

"Shee-it," Tommy whispered. "That boot-camp L-T is goin' to get us killed. Fuck him."

The lieutenant approached us. "How are you feeling, Doc?"

"I'll be alright." I tossed the salt tablets into my mouth and washed them down with water. "Give me a few minutes to hydrate. I'll be alright."

The lieutenant was not sympathetic. "I didn't know you couldn't hack it."

"Doc's got a lot of patrols under his belt," said Casey. "He's never fallen out, Lieutenant."

"He has now." The lieutenant peered at me. "You've got half an hour." He walked away.

Tommy grinned. "He's all yours, Doc. I hope you're satisfied."

"That doesn't matter."

"Leave him alone," said Casey.

"Why?"

"Because—"

"Hell."

"Because we've messed with him long enough."

"Shit." Tommy chuckled then glanced at me. "Sorry, Doc."

I stood up. "For what?"

Tommy planted a cigarette in his mouth, lit it with his Zippo then exhaled. "You're one of the good guys."

"He's the best," Casey added. He lit a cigarette, took a strong drag, and offered it to me.

I took the cigarette. "What are you talking about?"

Tommy grinned. "We weren't going to do it."

"You weren't?"

"I'll tell the L-T you're alright." Tommy ambled toward the lieutenant, Lima, and the assistant patrol leader who were sitting out this break together.

I peered at Casey.

Casey bit his lower lip. "We were . . . were just messing with you."

"Oh, nice. That's just great."

"Don't get mad."

"I'm not mad."

"Okay."

I took a grateful drag from my cigarette and gave it back to Casey. "Okay."

He took a drag from his cigarette.

The smoke tasted good.

The lieutenant gave the signal to saddle up as Tommy walked past us to assume his position as tail-end-charlie. "That L-T is a lucky bastard and he don't know it."

○ ○ ○ ○

Daybreak routine. I drank deeply from my canteen.

Early morning fog. I prepared my chicken and rice long-rat.

I stood up and stretched then found a place to urinate. My numbed senses always made me feel vulnerable at this hour.

I ate my long-rat, smoked a cigarette, and answered nature's call once again behind the privacy of a tree.

Nature. Consumed by nature in a foreign land immersed in a war.

For me, the war meant: being grateful when I saw my patrol leader exhale the smoke of a freshly lit cigarette.

I plucked another cigarette from the pack nestled in my left top pocket and lit it. The smoke tasted good; the war was on hold until . . . until . . . .

Our patrol leader planted what was left of his smoldering cigarette in the corner of his mouth and began assembling his gear. This was the cue that set the patrol in motion.

Daybreak routine was over.

◦ ◦ ◦ ◦

I did not know why our patrol leader wanted us to hump so hard and fast and carelessly. But he was our patrol leader and in charge and intensely focused upon staying on the move.

We were moving too hard and fast.

The staff sergeant did not have a combat reputation. He seemed too nervous to be a patrol leader. He consulted his map too often.

I was beginning to feel that we were lost. This was unusual for me, because I rarely asked what was going on. This was a habit that a corpsman could afford to have in a combat environment, a habit that a corpsman needed to have in order not to lose sight of who he was and why he was there in the first place: to care for the sick and injured. Some corpsmen forgot this principal and became more marine than a marine—more Catholic than the Pope. But a marine was a marine because he had survived boot camp at Paris Island—the place where marines were born, the place where a marine earned his eagle, globe, and anchor. I was issued mine with my Marine Corps uniform, and so was every other corpsman.

My training had been just as demanding, but not the same. Marines respected corpsmen because their mission to save lives sometimes required a special brand of self-sacrifice. Still, this made us part of them, not one of them.

The heat of the day, the weight of my backpack, and my growing fatigue was cause for alarm. We were moving too fast. Taking no breaks. Making too much noise.

My Unit One medical bag felt like a fifty-pound rock hanging from a strap that pressed down on my right shoulder, crossed my back and chest, and dangled cumbersomely against my left side.

What was this staff sergeant doing? Were we rushing toward a destination or were we running from something?

I peered at the M-79 man behind me and caught his bewilderment before he tripped on a vine.

We continued to push very hard.

The primary radioman gazed back at me with an expression similar to the M-79 man behind me. I stumbled onto my knees.

I exhaled. I released . . . I wasn't able to get up. I was falling-out. I was too numb to care about losing my pride. I was . . . I was grateful when the radioman turned to me again and signaled that the staff sergeant had ordered a break.

I relayed the signal then allowed the weight of my backpack to pull me backward onto the ground. I leaned against it and I contemplated a cigarette, but I was too tired to reach for one.

I stared into a wall of green foliage and waited for my body to recover. As soon as I had the strength for a cigarette, the staff sergeant stood up. His signal to "move out" forced us to our feet.

With unusual speed and intensity, we traveled without another break until dusk.

The terrain had been mountainous and the surrounding flora had been thick. As soon as we came to a halt, I dropped my backpack and sat on the ground. I wanted a cigarette, but it was too late to light up. Night was descending.

Suddenly, I noticed that nobody had reached into a backpack or had broken out a claymore mine. I was confused. Then I realized we were on a break; I realized we were going to travel into the darkness.

I kept my concerns to myself.

I was still amazed when I saw the signal to "move out." I stood up, put on my backpack, grabbed my rifle, and followed the man in front of me.

Shadows deepened into darkness, into pitch, into blackness, into—

I tripped. I heard others stumbling. We couldn't see.

When we reached a very steep rock-face, it broke like shifting gravel with each downward step. The noise of the tumbling rock and our crunching feet was frighteningly loud.

If the enemy had been here, they would have known our position.

Our position. What the hell was our position? I was blind and I was sliding down a sixty-degree rock-face on my rump toward what seemed to be the abyss.

"Let's stop here," said the staff sergeant, in a full voice that shattered my nerves.

I simply stopped gliding down the rocky mountainside and leaned against my backpack for support.

Now what? It was too dark to eat or smoke or pee.

I laid my rifle next to me then lifted the strap attached to my medical bag over my head to get free from the bulky Unit One. I unbuckled my web belt then slipped out of my backpack and web belt harness straps.

I sought comfort on my rock-bed for the night by rolling on to my right side and resting my face on my flattened bush cover; the incline was so steep that it was unnecessary to prop my head up on my backpack.

My thirst burned; I was too tired to reach for one of my canteens. My legs throbbed; I was immobilized by the depth of this darkness.

Nothing. I could see nothing. I didn't know if my eyes were open or closed.

A shock of light made me sit up. "What the hell?"

"Is that you, Sergeant?" someone whispered.

"Relax, relax," the staff sergeant mumbled. "There aren't any VC around here."

"What the hell are you doin'?" someone else challenged.

"Gettin' a fix on our position." The edginess in the staff sergeant's voice revealed his insecurity.

"Shit."

Someone growled.

"You mean, you're lost?" said Tommy, our tail-end-charlie.

"Shut up." The staff sergeant's bark invited the stronger members of our pack to test his authority.

"What difference does it make?" said our point man.

"Yeah. We ain't goin' anywhere now," Tommy added.

Several guys laughed. Their tone was menacing.

"Jesus," Dogen taunted.

"What?" the staff sergeant countered.

Several members of the pack responded.

"You're goin' to get us kilt with that flashlight."

"Yeah, Sergeant, we ain't goin' nowhere anyhow."

Someone snorted.

"Turn that damn thing off, you fool."

"Who said that?" the staff sergeant demanded.

Dark laughter was the threatening response.

Thick silence.

The flashlight went out.

Hard silence.

The pack exhaled slowly in an effort to relax from this insanity. Exhaustion prevailed.

Plain silence.

I fell asleep hoping that my throat would not be cut that night.

○ ○ ○ ○

Two days on patrol without enemy contact.

The mountainous region made travel slow and difficult. We humped. We plodded. We reached a strange portal—its passageway appeared to penetrate the face of a mountain.

We hesitated before proceeding through this passageway.

As soon as I reached the other side, I felt calm. I stepped onto a large flat rock, which extended toward the bottom of a waterfall. The silence of the falling water was mesmerizing; the depth of this green place was enchanting. Captivating. Disarming.

I lifted the strap of my Unit One off my shoulder and over my head then I set the bag on the ground and propped my rifle against it. I dropped my backpack, unbuckled my web belt, and placed the weight of my ammo pouches and canteens on the ground. I noticed that everybody else had done the same thing.

Calm presided over us.

The floor of this green place was a flat square rock, which projected over a large pool of water at the bottom of the waterfall. This space was defined by a waterfall with a wall of vegetation on both sides. In the place where a fourth wall would have been, there was a ledge that presented a panoramic view of the mountainous region.

I looked up. There was no sky. I should have been afraid but I wasn't. Instead, I was amused when I heard voices and laughter and the splash of water.

Lima was already swimming in the pool; his gear and clothes were stacked by the pool's edge.

Tommy Bolton was naked. "Doc, don't just stand there."

"The water's like silk!" Lima shouted.

Somehow we knew we were safe here.

We became immersed in this magical place, this protected place, this place where the war stood still.

I sat down near the edge of the pool and unlaced my boots before I lit a cigarette. The smoke tasted clean.

I pulled off my boots and socks, raised my trousers above my knees, and submerged my feet into the water.

Silk.

I studied my feet. The clear water had no temperature.

Insane.

I looked around and saw abandoned gear, discarded weapons, strewn clothing, and naked men swimming and lounging and smoking and drifting carelessly.

I stared at the waterfall. Clear. Clean. Real.

Horseplay punctuated the indescribable magic of this protected place.

As soon as I took off my clothes, two guys picked me up and threw me into the water. Laughter greeted me when I came to the surface.

We played in heaven for an undetermined period of time. Then, without a single command, we simply got dressed, saddled up, and got into formation. No one spoke.

We approached the interior side of the portal, entered the passageway, and walked back into our dimension. As soon as we passed through the exterior side of the portal, the weight of the present erased my lightness. We were back in the war.

oooo

Sudden fall. A figure. An ordinary shot. I killed him.

I felt—neutral. Ordinary. The moment did not emotionally engage me. I was surprised.

We had made contact.

A silhouette appeared and demanded my attention. I had taken aim.

Bam. Bam bam.

The silhouette had stiffened then disappeared.

In a blink of an eye. It happened. In a blink of an eye. I didn't want to know. I did not want a confirmed kill.

"Corpsman!"

I lowered my M-16.

"Corpsman!"

Someone was hit.

"Corpsman!"

I hurried toward the wounded man.

oooo

We were on a mountaintop. We monitored NVA troop movement proceeding toward an unknown destination.

I sat beside my gear and stretched my legs. Then I opened the top of my backpack and took out a chicken and rice.

I opened my long-rat, poured water into the clear plastic bag, and stirred the brown concoction with my white plastic spoon. Life was good.

We dropped naval gunfire on those troops below as I ate my cold chicken and rice.

I studied the remains of my meal as I listened to my patrol leader continuing to feed the adjusted target coordinates into the radio's handset. I lit a cigarette and took a deep drag.

For me, this was a picnic, not a fire mission.

```
Operation Order: 651-68    1st Reconnaissance
BN
Patrol:Night Hawk, Co. "A"     Da Nang, RVN
Debriefer: GYSGT Brenner           091450H
July 1969
Maps: Vietnam 1:50,000 AMS L7014
Sheet 6640 III
```

Patrol Report

```
1. Size, Composition, and Equipment
   A. Composition: 1 OFF, 7 ENL, 1 USN
   B. Special Attachments: None
   C. Comm and Observation Equip: 2 PRC-
      25's, 1 7 x 50
   D. Special Equipment: 1 M-79, 1 M-14,
      4 Claymores

2. Mission: Conduct Reconnaissance and
Surveillance Operations with assigned haven
to detect possible VC/NVA Troop movement
or arms infiltration with special emphasis
to locate and monitor enemy transit and
supply routes, base camps, supply caches,
rocket sites, and lines of communication.
```

Be prepared to call and adjust Air/Arty on
all targets of opportunity.

3. Time of Departure and Return:
071000H/091100H

4. Route: See attached overlay.

5. This patrol covered a period of 49
hours with 4 sightings of an undetermined
size enemy force and 3 contacts with VC/
NVA. Patrol utilized small arms, resulting
in 4 confirmed VC/NVA KIA. Team utilized
supporting arms calling AO, Gunships,
Fixed-wing and Arty Mission with good coverage of target. The team was inserted by
helo and extracted by ladder.

6. Observation of enemy and terrain:

A. Enemy: 071000H VIC at 902210 Team
traveled West Northwest on a trail. Found
a harbor site with structures and 4 campfire sites.

071315H VIC at 897313 Team found 2 booby
traps on trail. First booby trap was made
out of M-26 grenade with a trip wire
device, and the second booby trap was an
M-79 HE round implaced in the middle of
trail as a pressure type. Team disarmed
both booby traps.

080800H VIC at 887313 Team moved west
Northwest along trail. Found 3 fighting
holes that were reinforced with logs.
Sighted 5 VC wearing black PJ's carrying packs and armed with rifles moving

southwest. AO worked over the area with
good coverage of target. Team could not
observe results due to terrain.

090800H VIC at 883326 Team was moving
North along a trail. Approached an NVA
wearing grey flannel shirt and shorts, and
armed with an AK-47 rifle. The enemy was
sitting on the trail with his gear on
the ground. Team grabbed the enemy after
hollering Dung Lai, Chieu Hoi. The NVA
laughed and talked excitedly. Tried to
silence him by butting him with a rifle,
then fired a round in the air. The POW's
gear consisted of a cartridge belt with
U.S. canteen and M-14 pouch containing
a battle dressing, a bar of soap, and a
fishing line. His backpack contained food,
a cooking pot, a hammock and a pair of
black PJ's. Documents were found in pocket
of shorts. Team moved south with the POW
and called for an AO. At 0820H Tail end
Charlie observed 5 NVA wearing the same
type of clothing as the POW and carrying AK-47 rifles pursuing the team. While
engaging the enemy with small arms fire,
the POW attempted to escape. The point
man shot and killed the escaping enemy.
The APL opened fire on the 5 NVA pursuing the team in the initial contact and
killed one of them. The team ran to the
top of a hill, then ran down into a valley
and up another hill to evade the enemy,
but approximately 15 enemy, wearing grey
flannel uniforms and carrying AK-47 rifles,
were observed pursuing the team. Tail end
Charlie opened fire and shot and killed two

of the enemy. The team reached the hilltop
VIC at 878318 and set up a 360 defensive
position at a ladder zone. The AO arrived
on station at 0820H and began working out
with his onboard ordnance. After the team
established its position on the hilltop,
AO called in fixed-wing with 3 flights of
close air support to the north, northeast,
and northwest utilizing napalm and heavy
bombs on the target area marked by the AO.
Gunships arrived at 0900H and began working 360 around the team's position until
the extract helo's arrived. The team was
extracted at 0915H by ladder under heavy
small arms fire.

B. Terrain: Area was generally steep with
60-70' canopy and with thick secondary growth of 8-10' consisting of vines,
shrubs, bamboo, elephant grass, and briar
bushes. Movement in the area was difficult
to moderate. Water was available. Animal
life consisted of snakes, squirrels, rock
apes, birds, leeches, and insects.

7. Other Information: Insert LZ VIC at
908108 was poor. One helo LZ on hilltop
with 4' elephant grass. Best helo approach
to LZ from the East or West. Extract by
ladder VIC at 878318. Communication within
patrol area was poor due to terrain. There
were no OP's in the area.

8. Results of encounters with the enemy:
4 enemy KIA; 1 AK-47 rifle, 1 cartridge
belt, 1 pack, and 3 documents captured.

9. Condition of the patrol: Good.

10. Conclusions and recommendations:
A previous team patrolling this area
reported a base camp VIC at 891317. This
was the direction from which the enemy was
moving away from. Patrol leader indicates
that this area is a good place for a prisoner snatch or for an area bombardment.

11. Effectiveness of supporting arms:
Good coverage of the target area with
unknown results.

12. Comments by the debriefer: none

13. Patrol members:

Sgt Deitrick	2594802
CPL Norton	2497119
CPL McDuggal	2699082
LCPL Rens	9204813
PFC Lima	2381660
LCPL Bolton	2513414
PFC Dogen	2563086
HM3 Lenares	B334220
LCPL Casey	9364590

33

O --Insert LZ
X --Extract LZ
□ --Base Camp

X

92

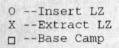

The above was the official Patrol Report. What follows below is the story.

Sergeant Deitrick was our patrol leader. There were several men in this team that had been on my first patrol. This was a rare occurrence since corpsmen jumped from team to team within their assigned company. I glanced at Sergeant Deitrick as our chopper banked steeply toward our insert destination.

On the opposite side and to my right, the sergeant sat on an unpadded bench comprised of a nylon material stretched across an aluminum frame that was attached to the chopper's bulkhead. Deitrick was a no-nonsense NCO who was planning a career in the Marine Corps. He was an ambitious young lifer who wanted to make staff sergeant yesterday, even though the Marine Corps generally thought in terms of tomorrow. He had numerous patrols to his credit. However, he had a reputation for being too cautious and a disposition for operating too close to the book. He was a tall and lanky Californian who grinned uneasily in place of laughter. He did not smoke or drink a lot or party with the boys between patrols.

Our chopper landed without hesitation and without the need for her escort gunships to prep the area surrounding the insert LZ with their air to land ordnance. The Hueys and Cobras flew menacingly in a tight circle hunting for the enemy in order to protect the CH-46 as we disembarked from the aft ramp of the idling transport.

We hustled away from the rotor's danger zone, formed a three-sixty, and waited for possible enemy contact as our chopper took off.

The formidable presence of the gunships above us boosted our confidence then they abandoned us. Silence followed.

I never liked the vacancy of this forsaken moment. I felt jettisoned from society, marooned in a dangerous land; I felt cast away, derelict—deserted. Waiting grew harder.

Deitrick stood up and gave us the signal to move out.

I rose with the others and got into formation by stepping behind Dogen.

We pushed through the elephant grass until we intersected a trail then hesitated before proceeding up a slope where we discovered an enemy harbor site.

A half-dozen thatched structures were clustered in a rough circle inside a thick network of trees and shrubs. Within the circle there were cold campfires and numerous abandoned clay pots and bamboo baskets.

We ambled around the area like lost children looking for something to break. Lima and McDuggal entered one of the huts; Rens and Bolton disappeared behind one of the structures. I wandered about with Deitrick and Dogen.

Norton smashed a large clay pot with the butt of his M-79.

"Why did you do that, Red?"

He was puzzled by my inquiry. "We're in a war, remember?"

I was confused by his answer. I studied the clay shards. "I didn't know we were fighting pots." I glanced at Casey.

"What?" Casey grimaced.

"Everything is dangerous here." Red smashed another pot with his M-79. "Everything, Doc." He meandered toward one of the unoccupied structures as Rens and Bolton reappeared.

Bolton lit a cigarette. "Are we burnin' down this place, Sergeant?"

Dietrick did not raise his eyes from the map he was studying. "Nah."

"Mormon thinks we should burn the place."

Mormon nudged Bolton. "No, I don't."

Dietrick smirked. "Stop clowning around, Bolton." He studied his map. "No burning."

Red entered a tiny hut as Lima and McDuggal emerged from the larger one they had searched.

"Abandoned," said McDuggal. "Nothing of value left behind."

Dietrick folded his map and stuffed it into his right leg pocket. "Let's push on up the trail."

Lima tipped over a tall pot and caused it to shatter against a flat rock.

"What are you doin'?" said Casey.

"What?"

"Doc here don't want you tearin' up Vietnam."

"Fuck you," I said.

Casey grinned. "I'm just funnin' you."

"Yeah, yeah."

Red emerged from the door of the tiny hooch.

"Let's go," said Dietrick.

We humped for about an hour before Lima brought us to a halt. Dietrick hustled toward him while the rest of us stood by.

After serious consultation with Lima, Dietrick waved at McDuggal to join them. Lima was on his knees inspecting something on the ground by the time McDuggal reached them.

"Booby trap," Casey whispered, as he approached me from behind. "It's got to be."

It was.

Dietrick waved at us.

"Get down," said Casey.

I knelt down and I studied Lima and Dietrick. I knew they were sweating because I was sweating from the heat and the humidity and the tension. Disarming a booby trap was the most dangerous thing to do in this world.

Lima ran his hand a short distance across the trail.

"Trip wire," Casey whispered.

"Whoa." I bit my lower lip.

"Yeah. It would have gotten us."

"How did Lima know?"

"He ain't Apache for nothin'. He's the best point man in the outfit."

"Damn."

Dietrick stood up then Lima—he nodded triumphantly.

"Crazy injun," said Red.

Casey grinned. "Yeah."

Dietrick approached us. "We're taking a break. Lima can use one."

"What was it?" Casey asked.

"An M-26 grenade with a trip wire device."

We did not travel very far after our break before Lima discovered an M-79 HE round planted in the center of the trail. The round had been modified into a pressure/antipersonnel mine. This time, McDuggal helped Lima disarm the booby trap. We took another break for Lima's sake.

I relaxed against my backpack. I smoked leisurely. I watched a lazy curl of smoke rise from the smoldering end of my cigarette. My mind drifted into the recent past:

> Jimmy barged into my hooch. "You're not going to believe what I've got!" He teased me with an envelope.
>
> I sat up on my rack and swung my feet onto the deck to make room for him to sit beside me.
>
> I was woozy from the powerful joint I had smoked earlier. I was still exhausted from the hard patrol I had returned from the day before. I

scratched my head, peered at Jimmy, and waited for him to read what was in his letter.

Jimmy slipped the letter out of the envelope and unfolded the page. A small white square of paper fell out and fluttered to the floor like a butterfly.

"Oops." Jimmy snatched up the butterfly and presented it to me. "This, my friend, is two hits of Purple Dome."

"Purple what?"

"Acid, baby. LSD. Psycho-delics, man. Yeow!" Jimmy showed me the two purple dots on the small square of paper.

Jimmy couldn't contain himself. Rarely was his joy so animated.

Jimmy was a fellow corpsman and my closest friend, even though we never went on a patrol together. He was a real bush corpsman. And his "hoo-ya" enthusiasm and readiness to accept a patrol assignment made him available and dependable, as well as popular and respected in First Recon.

Jimmy and I were very different. He was from the West Coast, I was from the East Coast. He looked like a hippie, I looked straight. He had a college degree in psychology from UCLA Berkeley, I had a high school degree in adolescent rebellion from Southwest Miami High. He was hostile to the military, I was indifferent. He was politically aggressive, I was passive. He had strong opinions, I didn't have many yet. He was pastyfaced and blond. I was Mediterranean and dark.

Jimmy did most of the talking, I did most of the listening. He was vehemently antiwar and yet: he constantly sang, "Happiness is a Warm Gun," went on as many patrols as I did, and talked passionately about every confirmed kill he witnessed.

I was drawn to Jimmy's contradictions: his hatred of government, yet his love for communism; his hatred of war, yet his love for patrols; his radical disregard for the establishment, yet his respect for First Recon.

His staple food was crackers with peanut butter, his drink was Pepsi-Cola, his brand of cigarette was Winston.

He ran hot and cold, happy and sad. He was crazy, and his friendship taught me a lot.

"Do you know how hard it is to get acid in Vietnam? Impossible." The paper fluttered at the end of Jimmy's thumb and forefinger. "As you can see, this had to be imported."

"From where?"

"California, baby. My girlfriend. Naturally."

"Right."

Jimmy stood up and peered out the screened window. "It's near sundown. If we drop these now—bam!—we'll be tripping with the stars in an hour."

I sighed with anticipation. "Okay."

Jimmy tore the paper in half. "Here. This one's yours." He reached for the nearby can of soda. "Is this your drink?"

"What's left of it."

He sloshed the can. "Almost half. Good."
Jimmy set down the can, trimmed off some of the
paper, and placed the purple dot on his tongue.
"Here we go." He drank some of the soda. "That
acid ain't going to do you any good in your hand."

I chuckled. "You're right." I trimmed off the
excess paper, as well, and placed the acid in the
back of my throat.

Jimmy handed me the can of soda. I drank
what was left of it then lit a cigarette.

I blinked. "Well." I imitated Jimmy. "Here
we go, baby."

And off we went an hour later. We went to
the hooch opposite the last hooch in the Alpha
Company area. It was built high on the hill facing
the main row of hooches. A stairway led to a porch
and a front entrance. The panorama of the rice
paddies below and the sky above was breathtaking.

We sat on the porch and gazed at the stars
and watched the M-60 tracers pierce the psyche-
delic night . . . .

I took a deep drag from my cigarette and crushed it out on the
ground. Lima and Dietrick caught my attention when they
stood up. The break was over.

The rest of the day was uneventful. We humped until an
hour before dark. After setting out the claymores, we received
our radio watch assignments for the night.

I got the twelve-to-two watch.

I ate a spaghetti long-rat and a coconut bar, drank a lot of
water and smoked a final cigarette. Then I stretched out on
the ground using my backpack for a pillow.

Night descended; immobility and stillness followed. Darkness beyond darkness cloaked our presence.

Dogen had the first watch, Bolton and Red were already asleep. Dietrick was whispering to McDuggal, Lima stared into the darkness, Casey searched for comfort, and Mormon was occupied by his thoughts. I grew thirsty again.

I unsnapped one of the canteen pouches and slipped a plastic canteen out of the musty smelling canvas. I unscrewed the cap and drank deeply.

I studied Dogen. He sat erect and still by the PRC-25 radio. He was a rock solid radioman who never became shrill in the heat of a firefight or a fire mission. Casey told me that Dogen never interpreted a message. He kept to the facts and never modified a radio transmission.

Dietrick separated from McDuggal and settled in for the night. McDuggal crept over to Dogen, whispered something to him, then crept to his own night spread and settled into the darkness. I glanced to my left: Lima was lying on his back and Mormon was curled up against his backpack. Casey had found comfort. He also had the ten-to-twelve watch.

I drank my canteen dry, screwed the cap on, and slipped it into its canvas pouch. I checked my grenades: I had two nestled in the ground on my right side. My M-16 was laid out on my left side and my claymore mine detonator rested between my backpack and my Unit One medical bag.

I reached inside of my backpack, pulled out a bottle of bug juice, and unscrewed the cap. Then I squirted the insecticide along my waistband, around my bloused boots, around my buttoned collar, down my shirt, and along the fly of my trousers. I squeezed some into the palm of my left hand, rubbed my hands together, and patted the bug juice onto my face like aftershave lotion. I capped the plastic bottle and dropped it into my pack.

Then I lay down, propped my head against my backpack, and pulled my bush cover over my face. I closed my eyes.

Fatigue assaulted me. My internal silence deepened. I fell asleep . . . .

A rough hand shook my left shoulder. I tore my bush cover off my face and sat up.

"Your turn on watch," Casey whispered.

I scratched my head with both my hands then stretched my arms.

Casey waited for me to crawl to the radio before he crawled into his night spread. The responsibility for everybody's life awakened me.

Radios intimidated me. Their message traffic generally sounded unintelligible. I was a low-tech guy facing what I considered to be a high-tech piece of equipment that required talking procedures that were difficult for me. I transmitted a radio check on the hour. The responsibility of the night watch kept me alert. Everything in this darkness sounded like the enemy to me. I was glad when it came time to wake up the next guy on watch.

Mormon sat up and remained still until he oriented himself. I had nothing to report.

He nodded and encouraged me to get some sleep. He crawled to the radio as I crawled to my night spread.

I sighed. I was free of responsibility.

I placed my bush cover over my face. I fell into a dreamless sleep.

I awoke with the morning light and with the urge to pee. I placed my bush cover on top of my backpack, stood up, and walked behind a tree to relieve myself. Afterward, I prepared a long- rat.

I felt chilled to the bone.

I stared into the distance and waited for the water to soak into the beef and rice.

I lit a cigarette, after my meal, and studied the exhale of my smoke.

Red disappeared behind a tree with toilet paper in hand.

I put on more green and gray grease paint. I smoked another cigarette. I blinked.

Dietrick gave the signal to saddle up. I stood up and got into my gear.

We moved steadily through the bush. The humidity was high and the canopy above kept us in the shade.

We came to a halt when Lima spotted five VC carrying packs and rifles. Dietrick got on the radio, set up a fire mission with an artillery battery, and directed them onto the target. We were not able to verify the results.

We humped the rest of the day without another incident or a break. By nightfall, I was so tired I almost didn't finish eating my long-rat meal of chicken and rice. I ached to the bone as I drifted toward slumber feeling the weight of a two-to-four radio watch ahead of me . . . .

McDuggal shook my left boot to awaken me. I sat up. I did not feel rested.

"Are you awake?" McDuggal whispered.

I nodded. "I've got it. Get some sleep." I crawled to the radio and sat staring into the darkness. I was numb.

The two hours went by slowly. Odd shadows jangled my nerves and made me jumpy; I thought I saw human silhouettes. My fatigued mind played tricks on me; I was afraid.

After Mormon relieved me from my watch, I felt like a child looking forward to hiding underneath a blanket from the boogeyman.

I returned to my night spread to snatch more sleep before daybreak. I felt safe with Mormon on watch. I felt safe with my bush cover over my face.

I fell asleep.

Morning routine at daybreak. Nature's call. Food and a cigarette. The signal to saddle up. The demands of the hump. This was life in the bush.

We moved north along a trail for a couple of hours before we saw an NVA resting on the trail with his AK-47 and his gear beside him. Lima and Dietrick crept behind the man and grabbed him. He struggled until Dietrick shouted, "Dung lai. Chieu Hoi." The man laughed hysterically then chattered loudly in Vietnamese. Dietrick told him to shut up, but the prisoner continued laughing and pointed a finger at McDuggal who tried to quiet him down.

Lima released the man, stepped away from him, and pointed his M-16 at him. "This guy is crazy."

"Bolton, Red; Mormon, Casey." Dietrick turned to them. "Secure the area."

The NVA's nervous chatter intensified.

"Shut up, damn you." McDuggal raised his M-16 threateningly then butted the man several times on the chest. McDuggal's ineffectiveness in silencing the prisoner made him angry and nervous. He fired a round into the air.

"What the hell did you do that for?" said Dietrick.

"To shut him up." McDuggal pointed his weapon at the prisoner. "See? It worked."

The NVA's eyes were wide with fear and silence.

"Yeah. Now every VC Charlie in the area knows where we are." Dietrick searched the prisoner. "Search his gear." Lima and Dogen kept their weapons pointed at the prisoner.

Dietrick found documents in the man's right pocket.

McDuggal found a battle dressing, a bar of soap, and a fishing line in the M-14 pouch attached to the man's cartridge belt. He dumped out the man's backpack and carefully rummaged through the items on the ground: some food, a cooking pot, a hammock, and a pair of black pajamas. "There's nothing in this stuff."

"Papers and a map here." Dietrick stuffed the articles into his left leg pocket. S-2 will have to translate this."

"Right." McDuggal snatched up the prisoner's AK-47.

"Let's get out of here."

"Which way?"

"South. Keep an eye on him, McDuggal."

"I will."

As we headed south with our prisoner, Bolton, our tail-end-charlie, observed five NVA pursuing us.

"They're coming up the rear, Sergeant!" Bolton fired at them; Mormon dropped back to assist him.

During the confusion of contact, the prisoner tried to escape. He pushed McDuggal aside and ran. Lima shot him.

McDuggal shot one of the pursuing NVAs. That stopped their advance.

"Let's go!" Dietrick shouted.

We humped to the top of a hill.

Bolton sighted fifteen more NVAs in pursuit. Red shot several HE rounds at them.

Dietrick called in the choppers and the fixed wings after he established our position on the hilltop. The fixed wings and the choppers gave us close in air support.

During the firefight, each of us managed to get into our rappelling gear so that we could D-ring onto the extraction ladder.

The enemy was all around us. We shot at everything.

The ladder hanging from the CH-46 was a beautiful sight. The chopper came directly to us then hovered patiently while we hooked to the ladder two men at a time. By the time the last two guys were hooked in, we were drawing very heavy small arms fire. Miraculously, nobody got hit. The chopper lifted us into the sky and flew us out of there. The higher the chopper went, the safer things got.

Red was hooked to the ladder beside me. "Looks like we survived another one."

I nodded.

I adjusted myself on the ladder rung that I was sitting on and checked my D-ring. I tightened my hold to my rifle with my left hand and tightened my hold to the ladder with my right.

The wind felt good. The blue sky was heavenly and the landscape was picturesque. Sound and color and movement was surreal.

I exhaled and relaxed into the wind.

Nine

THE PRIEST

I didn't know I was a priest. I didn't feel like one. But the frequency and intensity of men sharing their confidences with me awakened me one day: they were confessing their sins.

I did not judge their confidences, even though I knew there were moral lines defined by right and wrong that a man should not cross; there were consequences to all deeds because everything you did produced power in the universe and, therefore, was important and had meaning and was permanent. I felt sure that in this, my unsophisticated religious background was not dissimilar from theirs.

What supported my ethical geography was the heart of my parents' upbringing and the mind of the Catholic Church, which dusted my childhood with a spiritual awareness that was permanent, despite my mystical drift away from the church.

How could I be on the outside of organized spirituality and still be seen as a confessor? What betrayed me? Was it my eyes? My rating? My naivete? What?

I was no different from anybody else.

All the drinking and drugs and patrols, all the wildness of a young man let loose at the odd hours of freedom in a squalid city called Da Nang did not seem to provide enough camouflage to prevent dark souls from approaching me with confidences so revealing that I was paralyzed into listening. So active was my attention that their sins and minor transgressions passed through me like dissonant chords sailing through an unstructured emptiness.

I never knew when I was going to be confronted by a disjointed soul.

I was walking toward my hooch one evening when I saw the orange glow of a lit cigarette intensify because of the smoker's hard drag. The brief glow illuminated the face of someone I knew.

"Hey, Doc." The man stood inside the weapons cleaning station. "I need to talk to you."

"Hey."

"I need to talk to you, man."

"Okay."

Loopie walked out of the cleaning station into the moonlight. He was a short, dark, muscular Puerto Rican. He spoke with a Spanish-Bronx accent. He did not understand irony, or possess humor.

"Doc, are you listening?"

"Give me a cigarette," I said.

Loopie pulled out a pack of cigarettes from his top left pocket and shook out a smoke.

I plucked a cigarette from the cluster, planted it into my mouth, and lit the smoke with the Zippo lighter that I fetched from my trouser pocket.

Loopie waited until I exhaled my first drag before he spoke.

"I killed him."

"Yeah, well, that's what we're here to do."

"No, man. No." He blinked his eyes. "No, I . . . I think I did more than kill, I—" Loopie turned away from me. "He was a farmer. You know. He was working in a paddy and . . . and . . . ."

"Go on. Tell me."

Loopie took a hard drag from what was left of his smoke before using it to light another. "I . . . I murdered him, man." He flicked the cigarette butt across the Alpha Company pathway; the orange glow arced through the darkness and landed between two hooches.

"What do you mean, murder?"

Loopie cocked his head to one side. "Murder, man. You know."

"Talk to me."

"What I did." He planted the cigarette into his mouth.

"Go on."

"We . . . we were on patrol and . . . and if you had been there, man—Doc, if only you had been there —"

"Don't . . . don't say that."

Loopie took a deep drag from his cigarette; the smoke escaped from his nostrils.

"What happened?"

"We were looking to make contact. Any contact. The patrol had been a bust. We were bored and angry and tired. The weather had been bad and we had to stay out two more days because of the choppers. So . . . ." He took another deep drag. The smoke did not taste good. He pulled the cigarette out of his mouth. "So, we were looking for it, baby. We—I, I went out on that patrol looking for a confirmed kill. I wasn't coming back empty, man. I wasn't." He pursed his lips. "I was going to get me one, man, you know? You know?"

"Yeah."

A long uneasy silence followed. Loopie studied the darkness as if trying to understand the vacancy he felt within himself. "We got to a clearing, man—it was a rice paddy. And there he was, walking alongside a fuckin' water buffalo. Can you imagine that? Can you imagine that? I don't know what happened, man. But that fuckin' water buffalo pissed me off. You ever been pissed off by a water buffalo?"

"No. I can't say as I have."

"Yeah, well, this one did. Fuckin' water buffalo walking around out there like there's no war going on or nothing. Shit. And that fuckin' charlie, man, that fuckin'—"

"Calm down."

"Shhhit. Yeah. Calm down. Easy for you to say. You never killed a fuckin' water buffalo. You never killed—" Loopie rubbed his forehead with the palm of his left hand. "I hit my safety and yelled at him, you know: Dung lai, chieu hoi, caca dau. You know. Man, you should have seen the surprise on his face when I aimed my M-16 at him." He frowned. "Dumb son of a bitch. He should have stopped where he was and given himself up like I told him to. He should have stopped. He should've. I told him I was going to kill him if he didn't. Caca dau, man. Caca dau, man." He took a hard drag from his cigarette. "That fuckin' water buffalo—it started running. That VC's fuckin' water buffalo started running." His eyes narrowed. "I hate water buffaloes. I fuckin' hate them. Dung lai, chieu hoi, caca dau, mother fucker!" A crazed smile animated Loopie's face. "Then the guy started running—and he wasn't after no fuckin' water buffalo either. He was running away from me. No fucking way, baby. You're my confirmed

kill, mother fucker. Dung lai—stop. Chieu hoi—give up. Caca
dau—I'll kill you, you fucker. He didn't listen. That stupid VC
bastard was acting like a farmer, see? That VC bastard was,
was—well, he must have been a farmer because . . . because
there was no way he could escape. No way. But that dumb son
of a bitch ran anyway and I needed a confirmed kill and . . .
and there it was: my white star, painted on Charlie's Hunting
Club's roster at Company Headquarters, running away from
me. So. So, I wasted him." He sneered. "Then I killed that
fuckin' water buffalo. I used a full magazine on both of them."
Loopie closed his eyes so deliberately that it appeared as if he
were trying to control the madness within himself. He shook
his head. "What did I do? What . . . what did I do, man?"

I bit my lower lip and flicked my smoldering cigarette
butt into the darkness where it arced like a shooting star and
disappeared behind a shrub. "I don't know."

He peered at me. "You know, I murdered that guy. He
was no charlie. He was a farmer. I killed a fuckin' water buffalo and I murdered a man, and that does not rate as a confirmed kill in Charlie's Hunting Club. No way. No how." He
took a serious drag from his cigarette then flicked the smoldering object into the darkness. "There's no such thing as a
confirmed murder. No such thing, you know? There are no
stars for that."

"Yeah. Well. There it is," I said.

Loopie stared hard into the darkness. "There it is."

I was afraid to move or to cast an expression that might
be interpreted as a judgment. I wanted to be invisible more
than I wanted another cigarette.

Loopie was killed on a patrol a few weeks later. I didn't
know the specifics of his death. In fact, unless I was on the
same patrol with someone who'd been killed in action, I

usually avoided the specifics of a KIA and, if the specifics were delivered to the doormat of my mind next to the milk and the butter then I would quickly consume it—to be rid of it.

I wasn't curious about other patrols. I didn't want to know. I wasn't curious about the war.

I wanted my emotions to remain numb and distant; I wanted to prevent the aftereffects of violence from destroying my soul.

That was the worst of the confessions that I listened to during my tour of duty.

I went to my hooch. The lights were out. Several guys were already asleep.

I sat on my cot and reached for the pack of cigarettes sitting on the nearby shelf. I shook out a smoke, lit it, and stared into the darkness.

Ten

THE PARTIES

In the last hooch of the Alpha Company area, there were several pot-heads smoking marijuana and as many juicers drinking beer. The war made us brave about our drug usage; our officers looked the other way during our hooch parties.

"Wow, man." Jimmy plucked the joint from my hand, placed it in his mouth, and lit it. Dark smoke. He took a generous hit, then passed it to me. He coughed.

I took a hit from the joint. A lightness of being spread throughout my body and rested on the back of my mind. "Whoa. This is serious stuff."

Jimmy intensified the volume of the rock music by twisting the knob on the reel-to-reel tape player to the right then plucked the joint from my hand.

I lit a cigarette.

At one corner of the hooch, Farnesworth, Bolton, Smitty, and Schwartz formed a tense knot of tightfisted juicers clutching their beers and smoking their cigarettes. At another corner of the hooch, Dogen sat on a cot with Martinez. They were washing down barbiturates with a fifth of hard-to-get bourbon. Lima and Casey and Red staggered into the hooch from the Club, and joined Jimmy and me at the center of the hooch. They were speeding on amphetamines and alcohol and marijuana.

Red and Lima sat down on the cot opposite me and Jimmy. Casey stretched out on the cot across the aisle parallel to Red and Lima.

We were a motley group. Each of us wore pieces of our uniform: shorts and jungle boots, flip-flops and trousers, tee shirts or no shirts, and numerous variations of dress. Vietnam was hot and humid. Wearing less was always better between patrols.

TJ kicked open the hooch's front door and stomped inside. The door slammed shut. He swayed unsteadily. He was upset.

"Are you alright?" I asked.

TJ struggled for an answer. "Wasted. The stupid bastard got himself wasted."

Everyone shifted their attention to him.

"Which stupid bastard?" Lima muttered. "There's not a smart one among us."

"Yeah." Red wiped his nose with the back of his hand. "The smart ones are back in the world."

Jimmy and Casey chuckled.

"Spit it out," Farnesworth demanded from his corner of the hooch. He set his beer on the floor and stood up. "Who's been wasted?"

"Waller. Tim Waller."

Grimaces and bowed heads and silence underneath the hard rock music was our response.

"That dumb shit," said Bolton. "He should have stayed in the mess hall where he belonged."

"Easy, Bolton," said Jimmy.

"Fuck him. He was a cook. He should have stayed where he was supposed to be."

"He was a Marine," Martinez interjected from the other end of the hooch.

"And now he's a dead one," Farnesworth countered.

Lima stood up. "He wanted to be in the war, man. He wanted to be a warrior. Everybody here can understand that."

"Still—"

"Lima's right." Red leaned back on the cot that he was sitting on. "He wanted in. He told me he wanted to be able to talk to his kids if he ever got married. You know: 'What did you do in the war, Daddy? I was a cook.' He couldn't live with that."

Damn—was everybody's sympathetic reaction.

"How did it happen?" Casey asked.

"That's the worst of it." TJ lit a cigarette. "Friendly fire."

There were several exhales and shifts in attitudes.

"What happened?" Jimmy asked.

"Night action. They made contact a couple of hours ago. When the choppers came in for them, they got their light signals mixed up. A nervous gunner thought they were coming in on an amber light. When the gunner saw green, he fired. He took off Waller's head with his Fifty Cal."

"Damn."

Several cigarettes were lit. An uneasy silence struggled against the rock music.

"Somebody turn that damn thing off," Smitty hollered.

Jimmy turned off The Iron Butterfly in the middle of playing In-A-Gadda-Da-Vida. "Now what?"

Red stood up and approached TJ. He offered him a smoldering joint. "Take a hit. It'll do you some good."

TJ accepted the joint and took a hit. "They said his jaw was all that was left." Tears rolled down his cheeks. "The poor bastard. He was really worried about what he was going to say to his kids after the war."

Red bowed his head. "I know."

"Now he ain't ever going to have any kids. What do you think of that, Doc?"

"I don't know." I shook my head. "I never want to know."

"The poor slob," said Casey.

"Poor everybody," Dogen added.

"Screw all this talking," said Lima. "Where are the sounds? Pass me a joint. Where's the party?"

Jimmy hit the button on his reel-to-reel tape and poured the hard rock of The Iron Butterfly into the hooch. Several jays and numerous cigarettes were lit.

With a smoldering joint planted firmly in my mouth, I eased onto the floor and leaned against the cot. I studied the other men. Their private displays of insanity calmed me: I was not alone. My thoughts were also abbreviated: I tried not to think too deeply or feel too intensely. Timmy Waller was dead. And now his death was over for me. I had no more room for him. And neither did anybody else.

There was no other way to handle death in this place.

I was going to spend thirty days on an OP—starting tomorrow. Hill 452. Starting tomorrow, I could stay high for a whole month.

Eleven

HILL 452, THE OP

Trang was his name, and he was an ARVN: a South Vietnamese soldier; a member of the Army of the Republic of Vietnam. Like me, he was sent to this Observation Post for duty. However, I was serving time, he was serving his country; I was trying to survive a war, he was fighting a civil war.

There were five other ARVNs who shared two large bunkers on the opposite end of the OP. We rarely mixed. The barrier of language and culture and distrust encouraged segregation on both sides.

Heavy rain splattered on my bunker's threshold. I glanced at Trang who was sitting on the ground with me before peering through the doorway into the night.

"We are prisoners of the weather."

Trang didn't quite understand what I meant. His blank smile was accompanied by an uncertain nod.

I stared at the flickering candle between us and felt the humble shadows dancing upon our Spartan background: a wooden ceiling, green sandbagged walls, and a dirt floor. My 782 gear and my hammock hung from hooks attached to the overhead, my M-16 leaned against the bulkhead opposite the open entrance, and several cans of C-rats sat on the dirt floor near the tiny flame.

Trang stared at the flickering candle between us and saw god-knows-what through his inscrutable eyes. His hair was straight and black, his Asian face was youthful. He was lean and bony and hard.

I tossed him my pack of cigarettes. He withdrew a smoke, planted its filter into the right corner of his mouth, and tossed the pack back to me.

I lit a smoke. I exhaled. I studied the melting wax.

Rain and lightning and thunder. Vietnam.

Trang lit his cigarette. He had been a college student in Saigon. He had dreams and family and hope of a future.

I glanced at a torn sandbag; it revealed a stratum of hard-packed dirt and rock.

Geologically, Trang's future seemed bleak.

We smoked and talked late into the moonlit night and nursed the candle between us to prevent losing our bunker light.

I looked through the open doorway of the bunker and pointed at the lunar sky. "How do you say moon in Vietnamese?"

"Tan."

I studied the bright lunar face above. "Tan." Then I peered at Trang's dark countenance. "Tan." I repeated the tiny word several more times as I kept glancing at both faces: naming the one above and acknowledging the one in front of me.

Trang nodded to convey his approval. "Moon."

"Yes," I said with authority. "Tan."

The tiny word brought us closer.

We talked and we laughed. We smoked and we dreamed. We continued nursing the flame until it went out. Then we sat quietly without a bunker light:

Our labor was friendship to
Keep the candle awake but
the flame went out with the wax.

There was nothing left to do but to go to sleep.

○ ○ ○ ○

I felt somebody tug my shoulder.

"Hey, Doc, wake up. It's time for your watch."

I brushed away Bowman's hand from my shoulder.

"Are you alright?"

I sat up on my hammock. "I think I was having a bad dream."

"Yeah. Well." Bowman grimaced. "You haven't been right ever since you came back from that R & R." Bowman placed his right forefinger against his temple. "What's going on in there?"

I smirked. "What time is it?"

Bowman glanced at his wristwatch. "2330."

I was grateful that he woke me early enough to have a quiet cup of coffee and a calm cigarette before my watch. "What are you doing up at this hour?"

"I slept all day. I'll make the coffee." He eased out of my bunker.

I yawned, stood up, then stepped near the bunker's entrance, cautious of the mountainside drop-off just two feet beyond the threshold. I peered into the gloom, unbuttoned the front of my trousers, and relieved myself. I continued my thoughtless stare into the gloom after I was done.

Bowman emerged from the darkness. "What are you doing?"

"Nothing." I rubbed my eyes then yawned. "Where's the coffee?"

"Come on."

We approached the light of the burning C-4 that was heating the water.

Bowman crouched over the small fire, lit a cigarette, and grunted when the C-4 burned itself out. "The water's ready." He tore open two packets of instant coffee and poured one, then the other, into each cup. He stirred both coffees with a white plastic spoon. "Here you go."

"Thanks." I sat down on an ammo can and stared at the muddy ground. "Miserable weather." I sipped my coffee. "Hot." I lit a cigarette.

"Ah." Bowman burned his lower lip on the hot edge of his tin cup. "Yeah." He moistened his lower lip with the tip of his tongue. "Everything in my bunker is wet." He looked at the sky. "I hope we don't get any more rain tonight." He sat down on another nearby ammo can and approached his coffee with greater care.

I gazed into the blackness of my coffee. I felt the warmth of the tin cup radiate into my hands while my thoughts of home radiated into the memories of my ex-girlfriend. She flooded my mind. I could not escape the darkness of my last encounter with her. I could not escape my first impression when she opened her apartment door to let me in.

Auburn hair. Green eyes. Gabardine dress. Beautiful.

"You never wrote back," she said.

"I didn't know what to say."

"I'm not the same person."

"I still don't know what to say."

An awkward silence. Her tired eyes. My pursed lips.

"Are you going to let me in?"

Linda stepped aside. I stepped across the doorway's threshold and entered an empty foyer. She shut the door and led me into a bare, unswept room; neither window had curtains.

Everything was on the floor. In one corner, there were three broken cardboard boxes with kitchen utensils and unfolded laundry. In another corner, there were open pieces of luggage with clothes spilling out. At the center of the living room, there was a telephone and a desk lamp.

"How long have you been living here?"

She walked into the kitchen. "A few weeks." She lit the gas stove and placed a tea kettle over the fire.

I glanced into her bedroom as I approached the kitchen—a box spring and mattress. "Would you like to go out and eat?"

She gazed hard at the kettle. She was pale and undernourished.

I slipped my hands into my jacket's pockets. "Are you still going to school?"

"No."

"Are you working?"

"Off and on."

I stepped into the kitchen. "What in the world are you doing here?"

Her resentful eyes assaulted me. "How did you find me? What do you want? I thought you were going to Vietnam."

"I'm home on leave."

"You got a cigarette? I'm out."

I grabbed the pack from the top pocket of my shirt and shook out two cigarettes. I lit both of them and gave her one. "You don't look well, Linda."

She took a deep drag. "I don't feel well." Thick gray smoke escaped from her nostrils.

My cigarette did not taste good. I let it smolder between my right middle and forefinger. "What are you doing to yourself?"

The teakettle whistled. She turned off the stove. "I don't hate you." She took a hard drag.

"I don't understand you."

"I don't understand myself." She studied the cigarette smoke as she exhaled. "It hasn't got anything to do with you and me. You understand that, don't you?"

"I don't understand anything."

Linda shook her head then sighed. "Go away. Please."

"Are you in any kind of trouble?"

"What do you mean by that?" The growing ash of her cigarette broke and fell to the floor. She harassed the cigarette by flicking the end of the filter with the tip of her thumb.

"I meant nothing. I was just—"

"Prying. Damn it, it's my life."

I studied the smoldering end of my cigarette. "It's my life."

"What's your life?" Bowman interjected.

I blinked. Only the cigarette was real. "Words from a girl I once knew." I crushed out my cigarette, set the tin cup on the ground, and stood up. "It's time for my watch."

I went to my bunker, got my rifle and gear, and reported to Teasely, who was talking to Bowman. "What's up?"

"Not much, Doc." Teasely was tall and thin and pale. "We've got a bunch of rock-apes playing around out there. I throw a grenade once in a while, just in case."

I lit a cigarette. "Alright. Take off."

Teasely nodded. "I'll see you guys in the morning."

"Yeah."

Teasely disappeared into the darkness.

My watch was located on the eastern point of the Observation Post. The area was reinforced with sandbags. A wooden roof, supported by three-inch pipes, provided some shelter.

Bowman sat down on the stool near the PRC-25 and brought the handset to his ear to monitor the radio traffic. He peered toward the other end of the hill. "Those ARVNs always seem to sleep well at night."

I dumped my web belt harness and rifle on the ground and sat on the stool beside him. "Yeah." I stared into the darkness while Bowman continued to monitor the radio.

I took a drag from my cigarette, relaxed my gaze, and listened to voices that came from the past.

"You've done something to yourself, Linda."

She exhaled cigarette smoke. "I know what I've done and I don't need you to remind me. I wish you'd leave."

"Are you in some kind of trouble?"

"No, I told you."

I took an impotent drag from my cigarette. "I love you. But I won't force myself on you." My cigarette was burning close to the filter. "Maybe you're right. Maybe we can't live together with these political and . . . and philosophical differences that have grown between us. I don't understand these things. I don't know what to do about them." I crushed out my cigarette in the ashtray sitting on the kitchen table. "You seem to know what you're doing. I guess." I ran my fingers through my hair in dismay. "Anyway, I'm home on leave and I thought it would be nice to see you before I left for Vietnam. And even if we can't be friends, I wanted to understand the things that have . . . have made you what you are."

Her dark eyes assaulted me. "You can never understand the things, the ideas, that have made me what I am."

I sighed. "I don't know what to say." I went into the living room and picked up a folded newspaper.

She followed me. "I don't know what to say either."

I stared at the meaningless newsprint. "What about friendship?"

She frowned. "What for?"

"I don't know." I was exhausted.

"Hey. Hey," Bowman whispered. "Did you hear that?"

"What?" I stood up. "Hear what?"

Bowman was crouched near the sandbagged wall. "Over there."

I tossed away my cigarette and joined him. "Rock-ape, Bowman."

"Maybe. Maybe not."

"Okay. Then pitch a grenade."

"Right." Bowman grabbed a grenade, pulled its pin, and threw it.

An explosion followed.

"What do you think?"

"I don't know." I sat on the ground and leaned against the sandbagged wall. Bowman sat next to me. Together, we listened to the darkness. But my past drew me away from the present. This time, my thoughts drifted to a letter that I carried in my wallet. It was a "Dear John" letter that Linda sent to me while I was at Field Medical Training School.

I no longer had to read the letter. I knew it by the very heart that was no longer between us.

> *My Dearest,*
>
> *I'm leaving you. And I love you. But that doesn't matter. We don't exist anymore. You and this war and everything— I don't know. I'm breaking under the pressure. It's not your fault. It's me.*
>
> *I know, I'm really doing it this time. I never seem to be satisfied until I mess things up. I'm sorry. But I think I know something now.*
>
> *Remember just before you went away to boot camp, when you and I were told at that party that we had bad politics? You laughed at them. But I thought: how can I have bad politics when I have no politics at all? Then I realized that no politics was the same as bad politics. So, I experimented, and I searched, until I joined a group. Radicals. Protestors.*
>
> *I know what you're thinking.*
>
> *No. Wait. I don't even know what I'm thinking, or doing, or anything. These people that I'm with are for everyone, together and equal and, and, well, it's ruining my head.*

*But I have to do this. It's in my head. I have to find out who
I am and what I'm capable of.*

    *Am I radical enough to destroy our relationship? Am I
willing to throw away everything? It's so hard.*

    I'm crazy. I'm sorry. We must never see each other again.

        Love,

        Linda

I peered at the serious tan, then at the careless stars—
their indifferent pinpoints brought me back to the present.

Bowman stood up. "Something's going on out there."

"What?"

"I think I heard something." Bowman peered over the
wall. "Pass me a grenade."

I gave him one and kept one for myself.

"Over there. Let's throw one together."

"Alright."

We pitched our grenades and crouched behind the sandbagged wall. The explosions of two watch-tossed grenades
did not seem to arouse anybody.

I grabbed another grenade. "I think I'll throw another."
After the explosion, I peered over the wall.

"You see anything?"

"No."

Sergeant Lasker startled us. "What's going on?"

"Nothing," I said.

"Then why are you guys so grenade happy tonight?"

"We thought we heard—"

"Just looking for something to do," said Bowman.

I frowned at Bowman.

"Well, stop it," Lasker ordered. "You guys are keeping me awake."

"Sorry," I said.

"Why aren't you in your rack, Bowman?"

"I couldn't sleep."

"That sounds like a personal problem. Don't make it mine."

"Sorry."

"Christ. The relief choppers are coming early in the morning to get us out of here. It's going to be a long day."

"I know, I know."

"Then cut it out." He peered at me then at Bowman. "Both of you." Lasker turned away from us and shambled toward his bunker.

"Good night, Sergeant Lasker."

"Fuck you, Bowman."

"Sleep tight."

Lasker growled.

We chuckled. We sat on the ground and leaned against the wall.

"I think everybody is looking forward to getting out of here tomorrow," I said.

"No kidding," said Bowman. "Thirty days in this hell hole is a long time. I don't envy the guys who are relieving us tomorrow."

"At least they're getting clean shitters," I said. "They're not getting the unsanitary mess that was left to us when we got here."

"Yeah. You did a good job on that, Doc."

"Thanks."

We lit cigarettes and stared into the darkness.

The first of my inhale smoke led me to the past—

I heard Linda's voice.

"You don't understand."

"Those people you hang around with . . . ."
I offered her another cigarette. "Who are they?"

"They're people who . . . who believe in changing the world. You know, to make it better."

"I'm trying to change the world."

"By killing people?"

"You really believe that?" I laid the pack of
cigarettes by the newspaper. "That's not fair."

"What do you know about fairness?"

"What do you?"

"Everybody should be equal. Everybody
should be the same."

"And these people you're with, these . . .
these radicals—you believe they're going to make
everybody equal?"

"I don't want to talk about this."

"What do *you* believe they're going to do with
people who are not the same?"

"What are you doing with them? You're killing people just because they don't agree with you.
I'm committed to an idea."

"That's what you believe."

"You're damn right."

I bowed my head.

She responded to my despair. "I love you.
I always have. But we're too different. We see
everything from opposite directions. It could
never work between us."

"I love you too. That's why I had to see you
again."

She faced me with an eyeful of tears.

We embraced. We kissed. A fragile silence held us together for a few moments.

"It's too late for us." Linda relaxed her embrace.

"I know." I released her and turned away.

The last of my exhaled smoke brought me back to the present.

It began to rain.

I crushed out my cigarette then pulled my bush cover low across my forehead. "Damn."

"What?"

"The choppers won't come in the morning."

"Have faith," Bowman reflected. "Have faith."

"In what?"

"In clear visibility tomorrow."

"Right."

oooo

The smell of coffee invaded the hill with daybreak's arrival.

I was neither the first to hear that familiar sound, nor was I the first to climb out of my hammock and stepped out of my bunker to watch them coming.

"The choppers!" TJ hollered unnecessarily. "They're coming!"

We shook the weariness out of bones and threw ourselves into the feverish activity of departure. We were glad to be going back home to Alpha Company and we were glad to be escaping the boredom of this OP—even though this meant going back out on patrols.

Twelve

INTROSPECTION

The bones of war stripped me down to the essentials: neutral mind, disjointed memories, unclear emotions.

The truth about remembering war is the inability to be factually accurate or objective. No combat veteran is able to convey to a civilian what it is all about—it's impossible. We remember glimpses of war, punctuated by actual truth. The memory of an incident is usually fragmentary. Sometimes these fragments are long, but they are never whole. In fact, a war story that is too whole is usually suspect. A story that reveals too much either comes from a man who wasn't there or from a man who has been beguiled by the myth surrounding his post war.

Remembering is one thing, collective remembering is another—it's not you, it's what others want you to be; it's not about truth, it's about glory. And that's never the true story.

Nobody should want to be more than the truth. Nobody should want the glory of war.

Thirteen

PATROL FRAGMENTS

Weariness deepened with the accumulation of patrols that blended into a surreal montage of realities, which began with insertions and ended with extractions.

Existence became an aggregate of days—

Before patrols: Team assignments. Patrol briefings. Gear preparations. Stagings at the LZ for departure.

After patrols: The contentment of cigarettes after arrival. The assistance of the armorers in taking off our ordnance. The security of reaching the Alpha Company area.

Recalling patrols: The firefights were over. I would have died for those men. What were their names?

◇◇◇◇

Fragments of patrol reports follow:

Faceless men are remembered through the haze of distended time and place—a little war at a time.

```
Observation of enemy and terrain:

A. Enemy:

Team discovered 1 booby trap constructed
with new M-26 grenade and rusty trip wire
tied to an illumination parachute from a
155 mm Arty round.

Observed 3 VC/NVA wearing black PJ's
moving north to south across a sandbar.
Enemy were carrying packs and rifles.
Team called for fire mission (C/FM) and
received negative clearance due to
friendlies in the area.

Observed 9 NVA carrying packs and rifles
and wearing green utilities, moving east
to west on trail into village. Team C/FM
with good coverage of target resulting in
5 enemy confirmed KIA.

Team sighted 11 NVA wearing green and
black utilities, with packs and rifles,
milling around. C/FM with negative
results due to enemy moving out of the
area.
```

The monotony of the morning's hump was interrupted by the point man's discovery of a booby trap. The patrol leader hustled beside him while the rest of us waited and contemplated a cigarette. The heat made waiting feel longer.

The assistant patrol leader signaled us to take cover. I sat on the ground.

I peered at the others behind me. Their stoic faces revealed nothing.

I shucked my backpack, laid on my side, and waited. I was startled when the tail-end- charlie scurried past me and approached the intense huddle of men surrounding the booby trap.

I sat up. I watched. I soon found out he had observed enemy movement.

The patrol leader and the assistant patrol leader left the point man with the booby trap. The patrol leader signaled the primary radioman to join him and directed the M-79 man to assist the point man, as he followed the tail-end-charlie to where he had sighted enemy movement.

I approached the men attending the booby trap and watched them defuse the ordnance: an M-26 grenade with a rusty tripwire. "What's it tied to?"

"A parachute." The point man studied the nylon material. "From an illumination round."

The M-79 man nodded. "Yeah. It's from a 155 mm Arty round."

"Why would they do that?" I whispered.

The point man lit a cigarette. "So that someone trying to retrieve the parachute would trip the grenade."

"Who would want that?" I mumbled.

"An ARVN, maybe. You know. These Vietnamese don't let anything go to waste."

I lit a cigarette. "What are the others doing?"

"They're calling in a fire mission against three VC. They're traveling south."

The patrol leader approached us. "You done?"

The point man indicated the ordinance. "Defused."

"Okay. Leave it. Let's move out."

The point man took a final drag from his smoke and crushed it out with his boot. "What about the fire mission?"

"Too many friendlies in the area. Received a negative clearance. Let's go."

I didn't understand the sudden urgency. I took a final drag as I approached my backpack and crushed out the cigarette with my boot.

Gray cigarette smoke clung to the humid air.

We pushed through the bush as if we were trying to meet a deadline. We did not go far.

The secondary radioman saw movement and passed the word up to our patrol leader. He turned around and approached the secondary radioman.

Everybody stood where they were and waited until the patrol leader indicated that we were staying.

The primary radioman sat next to me with the PRC-25 handset pressed to his ear. "The sergeant's calling in a fire mission." He listened. "Green utilities. NVA. Carrying packs and rifles."

The sergeant peered through his binoculars. He was still. He spoke to the assistant patrol leader and to the secondary radioman.

The primary listened. He spoke softly to me. "Nine NVA moving east to west on a trail."

A 155 Battery responded. Multiple explosions followed.

I lit a smoke. I drank some water. I waited.

Five NVA were reported to have been killed.

The patrol leader continued peering through his binoculars.

"Green and black utilities," said the primary radioman. "About eleven of them."

Again, the 155 Battery responded with a barrage.

I listened to the explosions and continued to smoke.

Observation of enemy and terrain:

A. Enemy:

Found 1 VC propaganda sign that was 20"
x 32", made of wood and supported by
bamboo poles, 5' in length. On one side
the sign read, "G.I., Neutralism Will Be
Appreciated." On the other side the sign
read, "Refuse To Fight And Get Killed."
Suspected booby trap rigged to the sign.
Team took negative action.

Discovered 1 booby trapped M-26 grenade,
with pin pulled, and nested in a C-ration
can. Can was secured to side of trail
by a spike driven into ground. Disarmed
booby trap by detonating in place with
M-67 fragmentation grenade.

Located a rice cache containing 450 lbs rice
inside 3 storage bins 40" x 46". Destroyed
the rice and brought back 1 lb sample.

Made contact with 14 VC/NVA moving east
to west along railroad tracks. Could not
observe enemy uniforms or weapons due to
darkness. Made contact with enemy ambush.
Broke contact and pulled back to Hill 119.
C/FM with excellent coverage of target, but
unable to observe results due to darkness.

Long monotonous days. Hunger aggravated me into eating a
cocoa mix during one break and forced me into eating a coconut bar on another. I drank more water than usual.

Too tired for a full cigarette. Three drags and a long stare into the green.

Scatterbrained. Had to find my bush gloves after each signal to saddle up.

On the ground. My gloves. Almost beside me. But not there. Until I found them.

Haphazard. Fractured. My mental state. Whoa.

Late in the day, we came across a sign posted on a trail. Strange.

We stepped onto the trail. This was a random encounter and yet, there it was: "G.I., Neutralism Will Be Appreciated."

"Who the hell is supposed to read that?" I whispered.

The patrol leader circled around the sign to investigate the other side. "Us."

"They can't be serious."

"It's all too serious," said the patrol leader.

The tail-end-charlie considered the message as he approached the sign. "That's plain stupid."

"Look at this," said the patrol leader. He read the other side of the sign: "Refuse To Fight and Get Killed."

The tail-end-charlie smirked. "Jesus."

The point man joined the patrol leader and peered at the sign. He lit a cigarette. "What the hell does that mean?"

The assistant patrol leader lit a cigarette. "Hell, I don't know."

The continued lighting of cigarettes punctuated the team's bewilderment and transformed this investigation into a break.

While the patrol leader wrote down the propaganda, the point man grabbed one of the bamboo poles supporting the sign.

"Leave that alone," said the assistant patrol leader.

"What?"

"You ought to know better. Look. That wire. It's probably booby trapped."

"Shit." The point man released the pole as if it were a hot
iron. "Right. Right." He squinted at the sign as if he were suddenly coming to his senses.

"Let's saddle up," said the patrol leader. "I want to take
this trail for a while."

The primary radioman grimaced.

"What?"

"Nothin'."

"What!?"

"Don't like this trail."

"Saddle up."

We weren't on the trail very long before our point man
discovered a booby trap.

The patrol leader directed the point man to disarm the
M-26 grenade that was hidden inside a C-ration can. The
grenade's pin was pulled. Dangerous.

The assistant patrol leader assisted the point man; the
rest of us took cover.

Then the assistant patrol leader withdrew for cover.

The point man pulled the pin from one of his M67 fragmentation grenades, held onto the spoon as he placed the
grenade beside the booby trap then ran for cover after he
released the grenade.

The M-26 booby trap blew in place with the detonation
of the M67 frag. There were several nods of approval.

We proceeded along the trail until the point man discovered a hole in the ground that was poorly camouflaged with
shrubbery. We huddled around the site.

"Check out that tunnel for us, Doc."

I was the smallest man in the team.

I dropped my pack and my web belt harness, my claymore mine and my gas mask. I took off my bush cover and unsheathed my K-bar.

The M-79 man approached me and offered his 38 Colt revolver. "Take this with you."

"Thanks." I opened the chamber. Six rounds. "Good." I closed the chamber.

The assistant patrol leader offered me his lit cigarette.

I took a strong drag, handed back the smoke, and exhaled steadily before I jumped into the hole, which came up to my chest.

"Doc."

"What?"

"You'll need this." The patrol leader gave me his flashlight.

"Yeah." I turned it on. "Good idea." I turned it off and slipped the K-bar into my belt. I held the flashlight in my left hand and the revolver in my right. "Banzai."

I crouched into the hole, found the mouth of the tunnel, and crawled a short distance along its horizontal path. Then I stopped, momentarily, to orient myself to the environment.

The tunnel was musty and dark and narrow.

I suddenly wondered how I got there. I was on my own.

I took a deep breath to steady my nerves then I crawled. I felt my way along the tunnel's darkness.

I listened carefully. I moved slowly.

When I reached what appeared to be a larger opening, I stopped. I fumbled for the switch to the flashlight. Then I steadied my breath and my revolver before I shot a beam of light into the void. I scanned the large space then scoured its dark corners.

There was no one there. There was no other means of entry. I entered the space.

I was relieved to see three storage bins with bags stacked inside of them.

I set down my revolver, pulled out my K-bar, and carefully punctured one of the bags. Rice.

I slipped the K-bar into my belt, picked up my revolver then made my way back to the opening of the tunnel where the team was anxiously waiting for me.

"What did you find?"

"Rice. Lots of rice."

"Anything else?"

"Not that I could see."

"Good job, Doc."

"Be careful. There might be booby traps."

"Right."

The assistant patrol leader and the patrol leader went into the tunnel as soon as they lifted me out of the hole. I lit a cigarette and waited with the others.

The patrol leader carried out a sample of rice for analysis by Intelligence, and the assistant patrol leader destroyed the cache with incendiary grenades.

We took advantage of what was left of daylight and hustled away from the smoking tunnel using the trail. We succeeded in placing ten minutes distance between us and the burning cache before we made contact with the enemy. Dusk made it impossible to see if they were VC or NVA. They were traveling along a railroad track—they saw us first and fired upon us.

We returned fire then ran off the trail in time to avoid an ambush.

Providence.

We had stumbled into their right flank. Contact.

Scattered, ragged, small-arms fire. Chaos.

Increased fire: AK-47s, SKSs, M-16s, M-14s. Shouting, punctuated by several explosions caused by our M-79 man.

We broke contact.

We made it to higher ground and formed a three-sixty defense. Then the patrol leader called in a fire mission that blew the hell out of the surrounding area.

We were unable to observe the results of the bombing.

We humped into the night until we were blind and unable to continue traveling. Then we stopped and dropped our gear and bivouacked where we stood.

Nobody slept. I couldn't. I thought.

I woke up at daybreak.

```
Observation of enemy and terrain:

A. Enemy:

Observed 6 VC bathing in river. PJ's,
packs, and rifles strewn nearby. C/FM with
good coverage of target, resulting in 2
enemy confirmed KIA.

Observed 8 NVA wearing khakis and green
utilities and carrying packs and rifles.
The enemy moved into a treeline. Team C/
FM with excellent coverage of target,
resulting in 3 enemy confirmed KIA.
```

I had not been on patrol with any of these men. Hmm. Unusual.

I didn't know why I felt uneasy.

We humped hard on our first day. On our second, we saw VC bathing in a river. The patrol leader called in a fire mission and killed two of the enemy. That afternoon, our point man saw NVA moving toward a tree line. The patrol leader called in a fire mission and killed three of them.

Blood lust. Our patrol leader was dangerously aggressive. A crazy New Yorker. A corporal who had no business being in command. He carried a pump shotgun. He talked too loud and too fast. The bush was too foreign for him.

Days past. The weather deteriorated. We ran out of food.

The choppers were unable to extract us because of poor weather and visibility. Morale deteriorated. Don't know why. After another day, we were no longer an effective fighting force. On the next day, the weather cleared. But Battalion Headquarters decided not to extract us.

We wandered ineffectively. Then one day, our patrol leader started shooting at the bush. No reason.

Nowhere to go.

The choppers finally came for us.

```
Observation of enemy and terrain:


A. Enemy:


Team heard what sounded like a 50 cal
machine gun firing approximately 3-4000
meters east of team position. Team took
negative action due to distance.


Team heard 3 single rifle shots (AK-47)
fired approximately 30 minutes apart,
```

approximately 2,000 meters west of team's
position.

Observed 5 NVA wearing green and black
utilities moving from south to north along
trail into harbor site. Team opened up
with small arms on enemy. Observed 1 NVA
fall, and moved up to check out area.
Found 2 blood trails moving north. Results
of contact, 1 NVA probable KIA and 1 WIA.
Harbor site large enough for 4-6 men and
was constructed under large boulders in
ravine. Found 1 fireplace in harbor site
with warm coals, 7 china dishes, 3 metal
dishes, 2 metal spoons, 1 M-26 grenade and
1 chi cam grenade in a bandoleer, 3 bandoleers of rice, 3 pin-striped silk shirts,
1 pair green skivvies, 4 pair blue trousers, 2 cans of fish, chewing tobacco, 2
bags of tobacco, 1 bag of rice meal, 2
NVA packs, rifle cleaning gear, 2 straight
razors, 2 candles, fuel oil, numerous
plastic bags and parachutes, 3 hammocks.

Team heard two single rifle shots (SKS)
spaced 20-30 minutes apart and estimated
2000 meters west of team's position.
(Possible warning or signal shots.)

Team observed a punji pit 8' long, 4'
wide, and 16' deep, dug across the trail.

Team heard 6-8 rifle shots (AK-47) fired
semi-automatic approximately 1500 meters
northwest of team position. Team took
negative action due to not being able to
pinpoint exact location.

Point man and patrol leader observed 2
hooches with bunkers underneath. Patrol
leader observed light grey smoke from end
bunker. Observed 2 enemy coming out of
the bunker carrying small black cooking
pots. (1 VC with long hair neatly combed,
and wearing black PJ's and white plastic
sandals. 1 NVA with short hair, and wearing green utilities and Ho Chi sandals.)
Enemy moved in a southerly direction,
then they turned and spotted team leader
and 1 member of the patrol. NVA yelled.
The patrol leader and point man opened
up with small-arms fire, resulting in 2
enemy confirmed KIA. Someone yelled in
Vietnamese. Patrol leader and point man
moved toward team's position. The team
came under heavy small-arms fire and were
assaulted by 2 chi-com grenades. Team
returned fire and threw M-26 grenades.
Patrol observed 13 VC/NVA wearing mixed
colored uniforms moving west to east down
a trail in center of a stream bed and
advancing by fire. Team returned fire and
threw grenades, resulting in 1 enemy confirmed KIA. Team requested AO.

AO (Hostage Pete) arrival on station and
the enemy attempted to jam the radio by
playing Vietnamese music and triggering
the handset. AO commenced working over the
area with excellent coverage of target.
Each time the AO would make a pass over
the area, the enemy would fire at AO. The
team received moderate automatic, semi-
automatic fire, and team received 3 chi-com
grenades, resulting in 1 USMC WIA (minor).

Gunships arrived on station and commenced
working over the area with excellent
coverage of target. Each time gunships
made a pass, enemy would fire at gunships
and at team's position. Observed tracer
rounds being fired at gunships and heard
what sounded like a light machine gun.

AO requested a flight of fixed wing. Fixed
wing arrived on station and made 1 pass
dangerously close to team's position.
Pilots were notified and made adjust-
ments with excellent coverage of target,
resulting in enemy fire ceasing.

Team Black Pepper was extracted by CH-46
helicopter without incident. The LZ's
ground consisted of 3-4' elephant grass
with hard dirt surface.

B. Terrain: Area was steep on the mountain sides and level in the low ground.
Canopy on the mountainside varied from
30-65'. There was no canopy in the
low grounds and secondary growth varied throughout the mountainsides and
low ground from 3'-15', consisting of
elephant grass and thick brushes. Soil
composition was hard red clay on the
mountainside and the low grounds, and
loose brown dirt varied throughout the
area (top soil). Movement was moderate
to difficult and restricted to the rate
of 75-150 meters per hour for a recon
patrol. Water was plentiful in the high
and low grounds, and was seasonal.

Dog-faced. Fatigued.

No sense of time.

The sun. The heat. The bush.

The approach of twilight. The surprise of dawn.

Heard a Fifty Cal machine gun in the distance. The team stopped. Listened. Sensed danger in the distance. We pushed on.

Heard a single shot in the distance from an AK-47. Somewhere to the left of us. We proceeded without concern.

There was a second shot a half an hour later. Then a third. It sounded like a signal.

The patrol leader seemed concerned. He consulted with the assistant patrol leader.

I peered at the secondary radioman. He shrugged.

We pushed ahead with greater caution.

The point man saw enemy movement going north along a trail. The patrol leader directed us into an assault position. There were five NVA dressed in green and black. The patrol leader was the first to fire upon the enemy. Each of us used up a magazine and the M-79 man fired two rounds of HE. The patrol leader saw one man fall.

We hustled into a ravine and discovered a shelter constructed under a large boulder.

"Hey, over here."

The patrol leader approached the point man. "What?"

"Two blood trails."

The patrol leader ordered the tail-end-charlie to go up one blood trail and the point man to follow the other.

I remained with the others at the harbor site. The campfire coals were warm. We found dishes and spoons and grenades; bandoleers of rice, clothes, food, tobacco, equipment, fuel, candles, and hammocks. This harbor site had been their home.

The tail-end-charlie returned. "Lots of blood."

The patrol leader nodded. "You think it's a KIA?"

"Maybe. He was dragged away at first, then carried."

"Mine was probably wounded," the point man added, as he approached them. "Footprints and blood."

"One KIA and one WIA. Good." The patrol leader peered at the assistant patrol leader. "Destroy everything."

We did.

We proceeded north on the trail.

Heard a single rifle shot from an SKS. Twenty minutes later, another shot. A signal. A warning. I sensed danger.

The point man discovered a punji pit dug across the trail with numerous punji sticks. If he hadn't stopped to light a cigarette, he would have fallen into the pit. He was vexed. Shaken. His cigarette trembled in his hand. He was rarely fooled by camouflage. Semi-automatic fire from a distant AK-47 further jangled his nerves.

The patrol leader approached him. "You alright?"

"They're all around us."

"Are you alright?"

The point man dropped his cigarette on the ground and crushed it out with the heel of his boot. "Yeah."

"I'll take point for awhile."

"That's alright. I'm alright."

"You sure?"

"I said so, didn't I?"

"Alright. Let's go."

We continued traveling north until the point man and the patrol leader sighted the enemy.

There were two hooches with bunkers underneath. One VC and one NVA came out of the nearest bunker. Each man was carrying a black pot. They walked toward us and discovered the patrol leader and the point man. The NVA yelled.

The point man and the patrol leader shot both of them.

Someone yelled in Vietnamese.

We drew heavy automatic and semi-automatic fire. Two Chicom grenades exploded nearby.

We returned fire and grenades. Lots of grenades.

I saw over a dozen NVA moving toward us. I got scared. I fired my M-16 with increased urgency. I heard the patrol leader get on the radio and request air support.

The NVA were all around us by the time the gunships made a pass over our area.

Three Chicom grenades exploded near us and wounded the M-79 man.

"Corpsman!"

I ran to his side. Shrapnel had hit his left arm and leg. Bleeding was moderate. He was not in severe pain. Shock. Mostly dismay.

"Is it bad, Doc?"

I cut open his shirt sleeve. "No." I cut open his trouser leg. "No." I applied battle dressings to both wounds and kept talking to keep him calm as the gunships above worked over the surrounding area. Heavy explosions. Intense automatic fire.

When the fixed wings arrived, they dropped their payloads dangerously close to us. The pilots were notified to adjust their target coverage.

The enemy fire ceased.

I hollered for assistance when I saw the CH-46 approach us.

The tail-end-charlie helped me in getting the wounded man to stand on his right leg: he supported the good side and I supported the wounded side. Together, we hobbled toward the nearby LZ where the chopper had landed. The chopper lifted off the ground as soon as everybody was on board.

I looked out a window. There was a mountainous region with a dense forest on one side and a flat region with elephant grass on the other side.

We were lucky. We had found an LZ. We were lucky. We had one WIA who was going home.

oooo

Emotional distance grew with the accumulation of patrols. Faces were blurred, names didn't matter; the wounded were treated, the dead became objects to forget. Whole chunks of time became missing in action.

And now, now I can't remember complete segments of who or what or where—only a few details: moments of terror, flights of confusion, the explosions, the chaos, the small arms fire, the wounded and the killed on both sides, the bush and the choppers, the bush and the weight of my 782 gear, the bush and the night. Pieces of a whole I learned not to remember while I was there, so I could survive into here, the now—and until now, so I could safely remember what I could remember, and eventually share the fragments of these events that I needed to forget at that time, in order to be here.

Fragments of events—each, a portion of a patchwork quilt; a tattered spread of many fabrics spanning a whole year that, at a glance, seems unified into a single design, but with a touch, reveals the rough tatters of separate days sewn together into a sad memory draped across a hobo warrior bound for home on an empty train announcing its tired presence with a long and lonely whistle heard by worried mothers and working fathers and . . . .

◊ ◊ ◊ ◊

I sat up on my cot in a cold sweat. My green tee shirt was soaked.

I swung my legs over the side of my cot and planted my bare feet on the plywood floor. I reached for my cigarettes and lighter that were perched on top of my locker near the head of my cot. I flipped open my Zippo lighter and struck the flint with its wheel. The fire illuminated the darkness and formed deep shadows.

782 gear drooped from the rafters like a thick canopy. Inert figures were sprawled in their cots and jackknifed into various states of slumber: Passed out. Drugged out. Lights out.

I lit my cigarette. The fresh smoke of my first inhale calmed me.

Cigarette. Soldier, sailor, marine.

Cigarette. The one comfort reliable under all weather conditions—hot or cold, wet or dry; available for all emotions—joy and sorrow, fear and anger; and dependable with most physical conditions—hunger and thirst, nervousness and exhaustion.

I snapped shut my Zippo to extinguish the flame. The darkness was not as deep as when I woke up. I still saw inert figures—men who were trying to cope in a place with no future.

No future. Yes. That's why I was awake.

I wiped the sweat from my forehead with the back of my left forearm. I took a deep drag. The orange glow from the lit end of my cigarette intensified. I trembled on my exhale. I realized I was going to die on my next patrol.

After smoking half a pack of cigarettes and watching daylight ease itself through the darkness, I suddenly came up with a solution: the dive locker! There was an open billet in the dive locker for a corpsman and I knew the sergeant in charge.

I stood up with the strength of this realization and started my day.

I took a leisurely shower, put on a clean set of utilities, and went to morning muster. Then I went to the chow hall for breakfast where I knew I would find Sergeant Jim L. Broom. The sergeant was a broad-shouldered, muscular man with a high and tight crew cut. His starched cover sat in a chair beside him. He was eating breakfast alone.

"Sergeant."

"Doc. What are you doing here?"

"Breakfast."

"Since when?"

"Since I heard you needed a corpsman at the dive locker."

The sergeant grinned. "Brother. That was fast."

"I need that billet, Sarge."

He stared at me for a long time then nodded. "Sure."

"Really?"

"You've got a good reputation."

"I do?"

"I've been told you're good in the bush."

"Thanks."

"Don't thank me."

I slipped my hands into my trouser pockets. "I need to be pulled off the teams now."

"Why?"

"Got a feeling."

"I see." The sergeant studied me. "Like I said, I've heard you're a good man."

"So . . . ."

"Okay. I can respect that feeling."

"Can you get orders cut today?"

"You bet."

"Just like that?"

"Come by the dive locker this afternoon."

"Great."

"What's so great? You're staying in combat for another six months. I'm not doing you any favors."

"Yeah. Well."

Silence separated us for several moments.

"Report to the dive locker this afternoon. I'll have your orders waiting for you."

I still had some doubt. "You can really do that?"

He drank some coffee. "I can do that."

"Right."

Sergeant Broom set down his coffee. "You'll be okay."

"Yeah. Okay." I didn't know what else to say. I was simply grateful for his decision to give me the only I Corps dive billet that was available to a corpsman: me. I was also glad to hear that I had earned a good reputation at First Recon.

Whoa.

I realized I was hungry. I grabbed a tray and got in line for breakfast.

Fourteen

DIVE SCHOOL

Sergeant Jim L. Broom was a big, brooding, intelligent man who had an undergraduate degree in geology and economics, and a pair of Masters Degrees in history and German. He planned to go to Germany and attend the University of Heidelberg to earn a Ph.D. in something.

This bona fide character would not accept a commission. He hated officers: their elitism and their general stupidity. He planned to remain an E-5 sergeant in the United States Marine Corps until he was honorably discharged at the end of his enlistment.

He was the NCOIC—the non-commissioned officer in charge of the dive locker. He was so completely in command of this unit that it never occurred to me to inquire who he reported to at First Recon. I never saw an officer on official duty at the dive locker. Their visits were strictly social—Scotch on the rocks or whatever with Sergeant Broom. He had a fully stocked bar, a refrigerator, a radio, a ceiling fan, and all the comforts of home. He had the bearing of an officer and the intelligence of six. Junior officers were intimidated by him and gave him a wide birth; whatever he knew, whoever he knew, he was too dangerous a thing to challenge.

Broom had a penetrating smile and an erudite manner that managed to place the elite on their guard. He did not tolerate the stupid or the ordinary.

Jim L. Broom amused me. He was a mysterious man who possessed esthetic sensibilities. He quoted Jonathan Swift and William Shakespeare. He applied algebra to practical problems. He was engaged to a ballet dancer who lived in New York City.

Instead of cursing at idiots and incompetents, he called them yahoos—the name of a race of brutes he lifted from the pages of *Gulliver's Travels*. Ironic twists and archaic invectives populated his deceptively simple use of language.

I liked him. He knew something.

He was responsible for sending me to the Diving School at the United States Naval Ship Repair Facility in Subic Bay, Philippines.

He was responsible for changing the course of my life.

○○○○

What an exhilarating feeling it was to be riding on an open bed of a Navy-gray pickup truck with several other happy guys. The truck sped on a wide road that started from the end of a runway where the C-130 had deposited us and was destined to end at a barracks that was going to be our home for the next few weeks.

The sky was big and blue, the air was clear and fresh. Despite my exhilaration, I cowered from the expansiveness of this unsecured environment. A couple of guys noticed my paranoia.

"Relax, Doc. We're in R&R country."

"Yeah. Nobody's going to kill you here."

"Just steal your money."

"Or give you the clap."

Both men chuckled. They were wearing solid green utilities with a bunch of patches sewn into them to identify their name and rank, unit, branch, and specialty. One guy was a green beret, the other guy was from an airborne unit. They both wore silly-looking berets.

Overdone. Army.

I glanced at a fellow marine. He wore a clean pair of camouflaged utilities with a pair of black corporal chevrons pinned onto his collar.

Understated. Marine Corps.

The marine corporal grinned at me. "Hoo-ya."

"Hoo-ya."

He reached for his cigarettes and offered me a smoke. "I'm from Echo Company."

I plucked one from the cluster that he shook through the opening of the pack. "I'm from Alpha Company."

We had never met even though we were both from First Recon.

The other guys also lit up cigarettes.

The smoke tasted fresh because of the wind that passed through us due to the speed of the truck. Life was good.

The truck stopped abruptly in front of a large wooden structure. Several seabags tumbled toward the front of the truck's bed.

The driver stuck his arm through the open window of the cab. "Home sweet home!"

We threw our seabags over the tailgate and over both sides of the truck as we disembarked. Then we tossed our seabags over our shoulders and strolled to the main entrance of the large transit barracks.

When we passed through the double doors, the sharp transition from the sun's heat to the coolness of the interior mollified us.

There were two rows of metal bunk beds with corresponding lockers that faced each other. Most of their thin mattresses were folded in half to indicate that they were available. I claimed one of the lower racks by placing my seabag on the exposed steel mesh that supported the folded mattress.

"I reckon we'll be issued sheets and blankets," said the Green Beret.

"What's your name, Sergeant?"

"Pete."

"I'm—"

"Doc. You're always Doc. Remember that."

"Alright."

"Did you bring penicillin?"

"Yeah. I heard you're dropped from dive training if you get the clap."

"That's what I heard." Pete turned to the others. "You hear that? Doc's got the stuff to take care of us with."

"Hoo-ya!" was everybody's joyful response.

"Hoo-ya!" I countered. "But let's get something straight. I'll treat anybody here with antibiotics—but you have to swear to God, and swear to your mother's good name, that you'll report to a medical facility as soon as you get back to your units and have a VDRL done."

"A what?"

"A blood test," I answered. "You've got to promise that you'll get a blood test just in case the stuff I inject into you doesn't do the complete job."

"I swear to God," said the Green Beret sergeant.

The Marine corporal from Echo Company knelt on the hard tiled floor. "And I swear to my mother."

"Hell, I'll swear to anything you want me to if I get a dose of the clap," said the Army Airborne corporal.

Laughter and cigarettes filled our spartan quarters.

We hit the deck running the following day at 0500—and on every weekday morning thereafter in khaki shorts, blue tee shirts, and combat boots. We got no sympathy no matter what physical condition we were in each morning, after too much liberty the night before: drunk or hung over; with or without sleep; near vomiting or vomiting. It did not matter. You either ran or you fell out. And if you fell out, you were sent back to the war, sent back to your old unit in disgrace.

So we ran with that bald-headed first class petty officer instructor in the lead. And he ran our dicks into the dirt. We started with eighty men and ended with thirteen a few hard weeks later. There was no tolerance for failure.

A man had one chance to retake a written exam the following morning and one chance to retake a practical test in the water immediately after his first attempt. Failure on the second time resulted in the man going to the barracks to pack his gear. He was sent back to Vietnam on the next available C-130 flight. There could be no sympathy shown for anybody.

The marine corporal from Echo Company blew the "ditch and don" evolution, which required a man to descend the deep end of the pool in complete scuba gear, take everything off, leave the gear securely on the bottom, and come to the surface. Catch a breath. Then descend to the bottom, put on all the gear, and ascend. One instructor observed the man's skill level and composure at the bottom and another instructor waited on the surface to inspect him.

All straps and belts and gear had to be properly secured
and functioning.

The corporal came to the surface in a tangle of tank straps
and regulator hoses, in a disarray of floating fins and a facemask. He splashed around in a panic and that was a failure,
which he repeated on his second chance. He was sent back to
the teams, back to a war that we were both familiar with.

I could not feel sorry for him. I was next in the water.

In the end, I was one of the thirteen who survived the
training. I was no longer a mere man, but a U.S. Navy quali-
fied diver; to be exact, an HMDV, a hospital corpsman diver—
soon to become a combat diver in I Corps, Vietnam, 1970.

When I returned to First Recon, I did not seek out the
corporal to find out how he was doing. However, I found
out that not going on the patrol I was scheduled for, prior
to securing orders for dive school, probably saved my life. I
was told that the team made heavy contact with the enemy on
their second day in the bush and sustained heavy casualties.

I knew I would have been one of them.

Fifteen

THE FIRST RECON DIVE LOCKER

Jeremy struck a match and touched the bottom of the flame to the pipe bowl full of marijuana. He drew on the stem of the pipe and caused the flame to disappear and reappear with each puff. He blew out the flame and tossed away the match. After taking a deep drag, he passed the pipe to Allen and floated backward during his long exhale.

Allen pointed the stem of the pipe at me. "I'll shotgun you."

I stepped toward him. "Okay, hit me, man." I guided the stem of the pipe into my mouth.

Allen wrapped his hand around the top of the pipe's bowl to protect his lips from the heat then carefully blew into the bowl.

Pot smoke filled me up, hit the back of my mind, then traveled down to my feet. Bam.

I lost control of my balance and fell backward. When the flat of my back hit the wooden deck, I saw pink everywhere and in everything.

Jeremy helped me to my feet.

Allen brushed off the shards of my shattered self. "Are you alright?"

I blinked. "I don't know."

Jeremy grabbed my left arm and prevented me from falling again. "He's alright."

"What the hell happened, Doc?"

"You blew the back of my head off. Damn. What is in that stuff?"

"It ain't the stuff." Allen indicated the sandbag full of marijuana on Jeremy's desk. "It's the amount." He submerged his right hand into the marijuana, scooped out a handful, and let it sift through his fingers back into the sandbag. "See?"

"He's right. I think we've smoked half a kilo today."

I reached for a clean breath then sat down on the edge of Allen's rack. "That's pretty mean stuff." I lit a cigarette. I blinked.

The interior of First Recon's armory shack was also the home of Sergeant Allen Kessler and Lance Corporal Jeremy Dickson. A low wattage incandescent lamp shined in one side of the room and a lazy candle struggled against the shadows in the other side of the room.

Two beds stood on the right and left side of the rear wall, which separated the living quarters from the supply room; both beds were covered with green camouflaged poncho liners. A desk stood at the foot of each bed, which delineated the living quarters from the admin office; both desks faced the front entrance in order to conduct armory business.

There was a refrigerator and a fan, file cabinets and foot lockers, ammo boxes and chairs, a reel-to-reel stereo tape player and a cassette tape recorder, comic books and log books, and papers stacked on all flat surfaces. The space was cluttered with ashtrays and paperweights and weapons propped near pictures of naked women thumb-tacked into the plywood wall.

Because of the side-by-side proximity of the dive locker with the armory, Allen and Jeremy had become neighbors, then friends. After river operations or bridge checks or body recoveries, I partied in the armory with these guys.

I took a drag from my cigarette.

Living at the dive locker was quite a change from the crowded hooch life at Alpha Company. I liked the semi-privacy of the dive locker.

Sergeant Broom occupied the front two-thirds of the locker and PFC Youngblood and I shared the rear one-third of the locker. A plywood wall separated these spaces. I liked the sense of autonomy that prevailed under Broom's charge.

"I've got the munchies," I said.

Jeremy tore open a large bag of M&Ms and set the candy on his desk. I scooped out a handful of M&Ms and popped several into my mouth.

Jeremy stared into the abyss with listless eyes. Allen simply stared. They ate M&Ms.

My abyss hurled me back into my most recent river operation.

The steps taken from the chopper's landing zone toward the river's edge were ponderous. The shoulder straps of the twin SCUBA tanks pulled heavily against my shoulders. I followed Sergeant Broom and PFC Youngblood.

We approached a company of grunts who had been waiting for us.

Their mission: to search for caches of ammo, food, and medical supplies.

Our mission: to help them locate tunnel openings along the bank of the river.

We were directed to go to the river. We were told that there was a Z-boat waiting for us. Our SCUBA tanks and canvas dive bags grew heavier with each step.

When we reached the river, we set down our bags alongside the boat, took off our SCUBA tanks, and set them on the ground.

"Get the gear ready," said Sergeant Broom. "I've got to talk to that Lieutenant Colonel over there. He's in charge of this operation."

"Okay," I said. I glanced at Youngblood. His eyes were still in a glaze from last night's partying. "Are you alright?"

Youngblood nodded.

I unzipped my dive bag, pulled out the double-hose two-stage demand regulator, and attached it to the high-pressure manifold that interconnected the two tanks. I rummaged through my bag to orient myself: swim fins, knife and scabbard, rubber booties, canvas coral boots, snorkel, facemask, weight belt, depth gauze, and life preserver. All there.

I stripped down to my khaki shorts and green tee shirt then slipped on my gray coral boots, strapped the scabbard knife to my left calf, and put on my life preserver. Then I arranged my swim fins, mask, snorkel, and weight belt beside my twin tanks. I tossed my clothes, jungle boots, and the holstered forty-five automatic pistol with the three magazine pouches that were attached to a web belt into my dive bag. I glanced at Youngblood—he was also ready.

We lit cigarettes and waited for Sergeant Broom's instructions.

The sun was hot and high in the sky. The water was murky. Both sides of the river were overgrown with shrubbery.

I finished my cigarette.

Sergeant Broom approached us. "Get the gear on the boat."

Youngblood stepped into the boat and I passed him our equipment.

Broom untied the Z-boat as soon as it was loaded. "Get in."

I stepped on board, grabbed a paddle, and sat on the port bow. Youngblood grabbed a paddle and sat near the starboard quarter. As soon as Sergeant Broom stepped on board, Youngblood and I pushed away from the shore with our paddles and dug into the water to make way until the modest current began to ease us along the river.

I glanced back at Sergeant Broom who was kneeling amidships. "What are we doing, Sarge?"

"Come alongside the bank as soon as we get near that platoon. Doc, you're going in first." Sergeant Broom moved toward the bow and took my paddle. "Get into your snorkel gear."

"Alright." I stood up and stepped toward my gear.

Sergeant Broom pointed to the right. "Snorkel along the bank and look for tunnel openings."

I sat on the rubber gunwale and slipped on my fins. "Then what?"

"Let me know before you go inside."

I spit into my facemask and used the tips of my fingers to smear the glass before submerging the mask into the water. "And?"

"Make your way through the tunnel and find the landside entrance."

I instinctively touched the handle of the knife strapped to my calf. "Okay."

"Be careful coming out of the landside."

"What do you mean?"

"Don't get your ass shot off by one of our guys."

"Now you tell me." I put on my facemask and snorkel, gave a thumbs-up then flipped backwards over the gunwale into the water. I quickly came to the surface and swam toward the bank of the river. I glanced back at the boat to get my bearings then I let the current ease me along as I snorkeled in search of tunnel openings.

Visibility was poor. I had to snorkel close to the muddy bank in order to see anything.

Roots protruded from the submerged land. Rocks dotted the underwater geography.

I submerged regularly to the bottom of the river; my training and experience made my breath regulation effortless. I searched for tunnel openings by hand as much as by sight; the moderate current made my progress downstream easier.

A hole of uniform darkness caught my attention and became more defined as I approached it. I thrust my left arm into the dark space and swept my arm from side to side for confirmation.

I needed air.

I rose to the surface with my right arm extended above my head to indicate that I had found an entrance. I gasped for air as I turned to Sergeant Broom.

He acknowledged my find. "Be careful!"

I nodded and gave Sergeant Broom a thumbs-up. Then I pulled my knife out of its scabbard and dove for the tunnel's entrance.

I swam into the dark opening without thinking about what I was doing and quickly came to the surface inside the tunnel. The space was dark and musty and silent.

I released the snorkel from my mouth and raised the facemask to my forehead. Then I climbed out of the water, removed my swim fins, and sat quietly for a few minutes.

Whoa. Alone. How did I get here?

I removed my facemask and snorkel and placed them on the ground beside my fins. Then I grabbed the handle of my knife and pulled it out of the scabbard.

I peered into the dark tunnel.

I tightened my grip on the knife's handle.

I proceeded along the tunnel on my hands and knees. I proceeded and . . . and . . . .

I don't remember what happened. I saw daylight. I emerged from the tunnel on the landside. I stood up and waved without caution.

Several smiles greeted me. I heard:

"You're a crazy little bastard."

"You did good, Doc."

"Damn, I almost dinged you, little buddy."

"Is that all you took in there with you?"

I glanced at my bloody knife. I nodded.

Somebody whistled. Somebody handed me a lit cigarette.

I took a deep drag. "Where's the Z-boat?"

One of the grunts stepped toward me. "It's over there. Come on. I'll take you."

My legs were wobbly. My hands shook. I glanced at one of the guys. "Be careful in there. I think there's . . . there's—" My mind went blank.

"Don't worry. We got it covered."

"Right. Right." I planted the cigarette in my mouth. "Where's the boat?"

"Over there, Doc. Over there."

Sergeant Broom and Youngblood were securing the boat to the shore when I reached the river.

"Good work."

"Thanks, Sarge."

Youngblood took the bloody knife from my hand and washed it in the river for me.

I stared across the water.

Youngblood extended the handle of the cleaned knife to me. "Are you okay?"

I took a final drag from my cigarette and flipped the smoldering butt into the river. "I think so."

"What happened?"

I realized he was offering me the knife. "I don't know." I grabbed the knife by the handle and sheathed the blade into the scabbard that was strapped to my calf. "I don't know."

"Relax."

I nodded.

The lieutenant colonel approached us. "We found a dead man in there. VC. Who's confirmed kill is that?"

Sergeant Broom peered at me.

I shrugged.

He nodded. "I don't know, Colonel."

"Well, none of my men have claimed him."

The lieutenant colonel lit a cigarette. "Doc?"

"He's not mine, Colonel."

"Hmm. Alright." He peered at Sergeant Broom. "Good work, Sergeant." He glanced at me and Youngblood. "Good men."

Sergeant Broom nodded. "Thank you, Colonel."

"Stand down, Sergeant. Get something to eat. You and your dive team will be here for the night."

"Yes sir."

I retrieved my facemask, fins, and snorkel before the cache of medical supplies inside the tunnel was destroyed. Then I helped Sergeant Broom and Youngblood drag the Z-boat ashore. Afterwards we secured our dive gear, dressed and ate, and claimed a bivouac site among the grunts. Broom splintered off with a couple of senior enlisted men leaving me and Youngblood to our own devices.

One of the grunts approached us. "Hey, Doc."

"Hey."

"What's happenin', man."

"Hey. What's happenin'."

This was pot-smoking code. Head code.

"Reefer," said the grunt. "Are you into it?"

"Damn right we're into it," said Youngblood.

"I thought so. I'm Ricky."

"Youngblood."

They shook hands.

Ricky was a pasty-faced guy who sounded like he came from the Midwest. His jungle fatigues were filthy and his helmet was cocked to the right. Jungle rot was eating the back of his left hand. He had two ammo pouches and two canteens attached to his web belt and he had an M-16 slung, muzzle down, over his right shoulder. "You did good work, Doc."

"I was up first. That's all. It could have been Youngblood instead of me."

"Crazy, man. You guys are crazy."

"What's crazy?"

"Right." Ricky indicated a direction. "Come on. The reefer's lit."

We followed Ricky out of the large clearing where the company was bivouacked into the thickness of the surrounding bush. We approached three heavily armed individuals who were sitting on the ground smoking cigarettes, as well as passing an overworked jay. The reefer had not softened their mood yet.

"There's only one lit," Ricky declared. "How come?"

"We were waiting for you and the Doc. Who's that with you?"

"Youngblood—the other diver," Ricky declared.

"Cool."

One of them stood up and approached Youngblood. "I'm TeeTee."

"Brother Youngblood here."

"Yeah."

TeeTee tapped the top of Youngblood's mulatto fist several times with the bottom of his black fist in an African-American ritual that Youngblood responded to by tapping the top of TeeTee's fist with the bottom of his. They ended the greeting by clenching their hands together in a modified handshake that used four fingers and no thumb.

Ricky nudged me with his elbow and indicated the two guys sitting on the ground. "This is Monster. And that's Angel."

I raised my right hand in a half wave. "Hey." Monster acknowledged me by handing me a lit jay. "Thanks." I took a hit, sat on the ground near Angel, and passed the joint to him. "Good stuff."

"Yeah." Monster lit a fresh joint and passed it to Ricky.

"What's your no good?" Angel's blond smile disclosed broken and discolored teeth.

"Just trying to get by," I said.

"Right on. You've got that right."

"Nice work in the hole today, Doc."

I peered at Monster. He was a huge guy with thick brown hair. His helmet was on the ground beside him. "You think so, huh?"

Youngblood and TeeTee joined us.

"Don't bogart that joint, big man."

Ricky coughed up heavy smoke. "Easy, TeeTee. There's plenty to go around."

TeeTee exposed his large white teeth with a broad smile as he reached for the joint that Ricky extended to him. "Didn't I hear somebody say this was a hard day?"

"They are all hard, brother man."

Everybody agreed. TeeTee passed the weed to Youngblood who took an eager drag.

I stared into the abyss and wondered what happened to me today? What did I do in that tunnel?

I took a double hit from the jay that TeeTee passed to me. The double hit knocked me back into myself, knocked me back into the armory's present where I passed the joint to Allen.

"Are you alright?"

The question startled me this time. I peered at Allen. "What's alright?"

"You looked like you saw a ghost."

"I thought I remembered one, but . . . ."

"What?"

"I didn't. I . . . I remembered going into a tunnel."

"And?"

"And . . . and coming out of it. That's all." I shook my head. "I can't remember."

Jeremy passed me the joint after taking a short toke. "Then don't."

I took a hit and nodded. "I won't." I leaned against the straight-backed chair that was usually parked behind Allen's desk and scanned the tight surroundings of the armory. "I guess I'm either crazy or I will be."

"You're alright."

"We'll see." I rested my gaze upon a dark corner of the armory and drifted back into that recent river operation.

The evening's swift approach had caught us off guard. Monster sat up with alarm. "Damn. Does anybody know the password?"

Hard silence.

Angel finally whispered. "Christ. No."

Youngblood grimaced. I remained neutral. The six of us stood up.

"This way," said Angel.

We followed him toward the company's perimeter in single file. We tried to approach cautiously.

"Who's out there?" somebody shouted.

"It's Angel—"

"And Monster!"

"Jesus! I almost wasted you." The man on watch was surprised to see so many of us. "What the hell were you guys doing out there?"

"Tokin' on some smoke, baby."

"You guys are nuts."

"Yeah. And we forgot to get the call sign."

"No shit, man. It's *Clearwater*."

"Now you tell me."

TeeTee and Ricky chuckled.

"You guys better split up before the lieutenant or the captain sees you."

"Right."

Youngblood and I splintered away from the others and searched the company area in the darkness until we found our gear. I pulled the poncho liner out of my dive bag and spread it on the ground. Then I lay down, rested my head against my dive bag, and wrapped half the poncho liner over me.

"Are you alright, Doc?"

"I'm alright."

No more said. Intense darkness. Restless slumber.

Explosions and small arms fire and men shouting startled me. I sat up.

Sporadic muzzle flashes pierced the night. I thought I saw figures running. I thought I heard Vietnamese.

I reached for my forty-five automatic.

Nothing. The pistol wasn't there. Or rather, I couldn't find it.

I panicked. I got on my knees and rummaged through my gear. I couldn't see.

I felt like a stupid boy. My world had been turned upside down. I was unplugged. Disoriented. Suddenly afraid of the dark.

"Youngblood. Are you there? Youngblood."

I stood up and ran. Two explosions forced me to stop and crouch.

I heard a ragged M-16, an insistent M-14, and a threatening AK-47.

Men shouted. I heard lots of activity, but I saw nothing. I stood up and ran. I collided with someone.

"Who's that?"

"It's me."

"Youngblood?"

"Yeah. Is that you?"

"Yeah. What are you doing?"

"I . . . I was running."

"Where to?"

"I don't know. And you?"

"I couldn't find my weapon."

"I couldn't, either." He started laughing.

"What?"

"We're screwed up."

Youngblood's laughter infected me. "I know." Then I chuckled.

"I'm not moving."

"Not in this darkness."

At the end of the zapper attack, searching flashlights and curious lanterns uncovered some of the night.

I took a couple of backward steps away from Youngblood, tripped, and fell back into the present.

Allen laughed. "Damn, Doc. You're awfully wobbly tonight."

Jeremy untangled me from the straight-backed chair. "What made you think you could rock backward on those chair legs?"

"I don't know."

Jeremy set up the chair and Allen sat me down. Then Allen offered me a joint. "This ought to help."

I took the joint and studied it. "Too much. I think I've smoked too much." I passed the joint to Jeremy. "Damn. I never thought that could ever happen." I lit a cigarette and listened to Led Zeppelin coming through the stereo speakers that were perched on top of the armory's file cabinets. The music helped me shade my imperfect memory of a bloody knife and helped me to protect a couple of corners of my mind.

Sixteen

ON THE BUS

I was sitting in a bus parked near a runway. I lit a cigarette and looked out the window: dawn was approaching.

I took a hard drag from my cigarette, held in the smoke for a long time then exhaled wearily.

I was going home on the next freedom bird. I was getting out of this place in one piece.

"Incoming!"

An RPG exploded on the runway.

We were ordered to get off the bus.

I did not hurry. I did not seek cover. I almost did not get off the bus.

"Get down, Doc."

I peered at the guy who was lying on the ground.

"And get my nice dress uniform dirty?" I took a drag from my cigarette.

"Put out that cigarette."

"This is only incoming, man." I pointed at the horizon. "Relax."

"You're crazy."

"I'm finishing my smoke."

"You're not thinking right."

I took another rebellious drag from my cigarette.

"Everybody get back into the bus!" someone ordered.

I climbed on board, sat down by my window, and watched the darkness continue to dissolve into a hopeful dawn.

Seventeen

SEPARATION

Okinawa, Japan was the first terminal stop on my long journey home by air.

An overnight transit barracks. Another kind of blur of faces and places.

On this route, there were two categories of military men traveling with orders: those going to Vietnam and those returning from Vietnam. We were not allowed to fraternize with each other. And, in fact, we were kept separated by a fence.

I didn't remember that on my way to the war, but I noticed it on my way home.

Those who were going were clean and wide-eyed. Those who were returning were clean and weary.

Those going were restricted to the base. Those returning could go into town.

Again, I didn't remember that when . . . .

I chose not to leave the base on my return trip. I think I was afraid to. A note of internal caution forced me to listen. I listened. I went to the Base's EM Club instead.

I drank too much.

We drank too much.

Talk was about the war—and about the world to come. But mostly, about the war and about each man's unit mixed in with that . . . that salty sense of relief that it was all behind us now. Still . . . .

All talk about the war was an alcoholic blur. Specifics did not matter. Specifics were not wanted.

Talk. Talk. Talk.

And laughter. And very little listening through the physical fatigue of it all.

I didn't remember finding my olive-green steel rack at the transit barracks—only waking up, rising out of the bottom rack of my bunk bed, getting dressed, and finding my way to the chow hall for coffee.

Orders stamped. Flights verified. Boarding passes issued. Air terminals located at Guam, Midway, Hawaii, Alaska, and finally, Long Beach, California where I spent a week on a Naval Base processing out of the military—separation, they called it, as if we had been married. I considered it a divorce because I could no longer live with that person—you know, the United States Navy and the United States Marine Corps.

Suddenly, I was a white hat sailor again on a Naval Base that was far away from the Vietnam War. There were no war stories here. I no longer wore a Marine Corps uniform with Navy insignias. I was dressed in dungarees and a white hat and I looked like an ordinary third class petty officer waiting to be discharged with the other sailors who had been taken off their ships to be separated from the military.

This was another world.

This was good.

I didn't have to think too much.

I didn't have to remember so often. The shock of my new and present surroundings was enough to keep me separated from myself.

Too tired to drink too much.

Slept a lot in the lower rack of a gray steel bunk bed.

Made friends with two sailors who were also waiting. Faceless. Don't remember their names or where they were from or where they were going.

Out-processing everyday on the a.m. and on the p.m.

They processed us out of the Navy in classroom-sized groups.

Reams of blank forms and partially filled-out forms and fully filled-out forms were presented to us—all requiring that verification of name, rate, and serial number.

Most of the time, I did not bother reading the documents that I was told to sign and date and initial since they always told us what it was we were signing before we signed.

I did not read my service record's page thirteen, which outlined the details of my war record.

All a blur—and starting to have quite a struggle within myself.

I did not understand this internal struggle. I did not understand myself.

I preferred the blankness of no-thought whenever I could achieve that; thought brought emotions that I did not want. I had managed quite well without them in the war, thank you. But now, here I was facing this . . . this . . . .

Separation orders. Airline tickets that would be stamped and augmented with boarding passes at Long Beach, Chicago, Atlanta, and finally, Miami, Florida where my parents lived— my only destination at that time.

Time. I had a lot of that on my hands these days.

I smoked a lot of cigarettes.

Eighteen

THE CLEANSING RITUAL

Two quarters, a dime, and four pennies in change. Change.

In an effort to comprehend their unfamiliar texture, I wiggled my fingers in an undulating fashion as I studied the coins in my left palm.

Lincoln. Washington. Roosevelt.

I shifted my gaze to the colorful wax cup as soon as the lady placed it on the counter in front of me. The cup was filled with Coca-Cola and crushed ice that was impaled with a white plastic straw. My attention was split between the change and the Coca-Cola.

"Anything wrong with the change?" the lady behind the counter asked.

I was startled. "Oh, no. Not at all. It's just that—" I presented my palm full of change to her. "I haven't seen change, you know, coins in a long time."

"Where in the world have you been?"

"Vietnam."

"Oh."

I ignored her flat tone. "Just got back."

"I see."

"Change. There isn't any change over there."

"That's funny. Then what do they use?"

"MPC." I noticed the perplexed expression on her face. "Military Payment Certificate. All our money there is made of paper: nickels, dimes, quarters, and half-dollars."

"Interesting."

I put the change into my pocket and picked up the drink. "And crushed ice. I don't remember crushed ice."

She seemed less impressed. "Yeah, well . . . welcome back."

I detected a hint of condescension. "Well. Don't."

"What?"

"Welcome me back. Don't."

"Well." She turned her back to me to emphasize her indignation then went to the other end of the counter where she refilled the stainless steel trays with condiment packets.

I was sorry I was so curt with her. I stuck the straw into my mouth and swallowed the cold liquid until the burn of the drink's carbonation forced me to stop. I went to my seabag in an attempt to get away from this strange irritation and sat down on a nearby concave plastic seat. I sucked on the straw again until I heard a hollow noise from the bottom of the cup. I released the straw and looked into the cup. I grabbed the straw and I stabbed the ice with it.

I stood up and threw the empty cup of ice into a trashcan, hoisted the seabag over my right shoulder, and walked around the airport terminal until I found an unoccupied storage locker, among a cluster of lockers, situated against a wall in one of the terminal's corridors. I opened the door, shoved the seabag inside, and watched the door swing shut as I reached into my pocket and separated the two quarters from the rest of my change. Then I deposited the coins into the locker's slot, turned the key, and pulled it out of the lock. I glanced at the key and verified the number stamped on its blue head with the one on the locked door before I slipped it into my pocket.

I wanted a beer. It didn't take long to find a bar at Miami's International Airport.

I sat at the bar and ordered a draft.

The bartender studied my youthful face. Then he noted the three rows of ribbons on my chest, which indicated that I had enough time and experience in the service to have reached the legal drinking age. He blinked then nodded. He grabbed a glass from below the counter and poured me a draft. "You just get back?"

"Yeah." I took off my cover and placed it on the stool next to me."

"There's been a lot of you come through here lately. That's Marine Corps you're wearing, right?"

"Right."

The bartender placed a round cardboard coaster on the bar and set the glass of beer on top of it. "But look, I'm sorry, I'm still gonna have to card you."

"Sure. That's alright." I pulled out my wallet from my back pocket, took out my military I.D., and gave it to him.

The bartender squinted at the laminated card then smiled. "Looks like your first beer is on the house." He placed my I.D. on the bar.

"What for?" I picked up the I.D. and inserted it into the wallet.

"Just turned twenty-one, didn't you?"

"Yeah. Last month."

"That's close enough."

"Thank you." I slipped the wallet into my back pocket.

"For what? A beer is nothing."

I picked up the glass and drank half of it as the bartender turned away from me to take care of another customer. I reached for my cigarettes, shook the pack, and plucked one from the cluster. I felt safe and comfortable. I studied the crowd of liquor bottles on the wall behind the bar as I smoked and finished my beer.

The bartender picked up my empty glass. "You want another one?"

I lit my cigarette. "Sure." I took out a twenty-dollar bill from my wallet and placed it on the bar.

He poured me another beer, picked up the bill, and returned with the change. The glass had a nice head of foam and my twenty had been transformed into a small stack of bills decorated by a tight orbit of small change.

I drank and thought and drank and smoked. "Damn."

The bartender placed another beer in front of me. "Are you alright?"

"I'm just mumbling to myself."

"That's an old man's disease."

I crushed out my cigarette. "What can I say." The cigarette continued to smolder in the ashtray.

The bartender leaned toward me. "See that lady sitting at the end of the bar?"

"Yeah."

"This beer is on her."

"You're kidding."

"No. Happens all the time."

I nodded politely at her. "She's pretty."

"It wouldn't take much effort to take her home." He emptied my ashtray.

"Yeah, well . . . ."

The bartender chuckled. "Think about it."

I smiled.

A customer demanded his attention.

I lit another cigarette, inhaled deeply then watched the smoke of my exhale.

"I'm not used to being ignored," said the lady who had bought me the beer. She placed her drink on the bar, handed me my cover, and mounted the stool next to me.

I placed the cover on the stool to my left. "I wasn't ignoring you."

"Could have fooled me."

I wasn't quite sure what to do with her.

Her makeup was cracking and her eyelashes were burdened with too much mascara. Her shoulder length hair was thick and brittle and sprayed into place—it moved as a single unit whenever she turned her head. She wore a black-spotted gold pantsuit that was so baggy that it looked like a dress.

"You like what you see?"

"I'm not always sure I see what I'm looking at."

She frowned. "What do you mean by that?"

"Nothing. I'm . . . I'm just not very certain about . . . about anything."

"Don't be a fool."

"What do you mean?"

"Being certain isn't a sure thing."

"I didn't say I knew anything."

She shook her head. "You're the worst kind."

"Of what?"

"Forget it." She finished her drink, slid off the stool, and went back to her original place at the end of the bar.

The bartender picked up her empty glass and wiped off the wet circle it had left on the bar with a towel. "What the hell did you say to her?"

"Nothing."

He smirked. "Nothing."

"We had nothing in common."

"Christ. She's common enough. You don't even have to please that kind to have a good time."

I had had enough of this bartender. "What can I say." I slid off my bar stool and screwed on my cover.

"Where are you going?"

"Had enough for now." I scooped up what remained of my money, but left him a decent tip.

"Thanks, partner. Don't make yourself a stranger."

I crushed out my cigarette. "I won't." I glanced at the lady.

She smiled. "Bye bye, soldier."

I smiled then left the bar.

I walked along the airport's corridor without destination.

A lady's voice announced an incoming flight. A transistor radio blared rock music. A small passenger vehicle beeped constantly as it shuttled past me. A baby cried out with discomfort.

I walked into a bathroom and locked myself into one of the stalls. Then I hung my cover on the door hook, sat on the toilet, and leaned my head against the metal partition. I closed my eyes and broke out into a cold sweat as I heard the sound of incoming choppers:

There was nothing more that I could do for him, nothing. Nothing.

"Concentrate on your breathing, Froggy. The medevac will be here soon."

The crater was half-full of water and both of us were partially submerged in a murky compound of mud, blood, and debris.

I held Froggy in my arms and tried not to
disturb his bandaged chest wound. He coughed
up a huge chunk of blood then exhaled his final
moment of life.

Despite all my efforts, I could not stop his
entry into the nothingness of death.

The monsoon rain did not wash away the dirt
from his face. I looked up at the small gray sky
and blinked in response to the rain.

This was not a cleansing rain. This was not a
baptismal rain.

I caressed Froggy. I couldn't cry. I couldn't
cry about a future that wasn't there.

I placed the flat of my left hand against the metal partition and pushed myself away from it. Then I pulled out a few
sheets of toilet paper from the roll and wiped my brow before
blowing my nose.

I grabbed my cover as I unlocked the door and stepped in
front of a sink. I stared at the day-old civilian in the day-old
uniform reflected in the large mirror. I tossed my cover on
the counter and threw the wadded toilet paper into a stainless
steel trash receptacle.

Somebody walked into the bathroom to use the urinal.

I turned on the water, bent over the sink, and washed my
face until the intruder left.

My wet hands remained cupped over my face.

I peered through the latticework of my fingers hoping to
discover a different image reflected in the mirror.

I didn't.

I pulled four paper towels out of the dispenser and dried my face, neck, hands—then blew my nose into the cool wet paper before throwing it into the trash.

I unbuckled and unbuttoned my green service coat and did the same to my trousers in order to adjust my shirt neatly around my waist. Then I zipped and buttoned and buckled myself up. I straightened my tie and placed my cover squarely on my head.

Again, I stared into the mirror. This time, I saw what I once was: a U.S. Navy Hospital Corpsman who was no longer attached to the U.S. Marine Corps or to First Recon—a man who was separated from all of the above and going home wearing his FMF Marine Corps service uniform for the last time. "Alright. I think it's time to get something to eat."

I walked along the corridor until I reached a huge lobby dressed with numerous shops and places to eat on all four sides of its perimeter.

I discovered a glass-encased room full of unoccupied tables. Each table had a white cloth draped over it, a delicate flower in a crystal vase perched at the center, and four elegant silver place settings with beige napkins pitched like little tents, waiting to be picked up and disassembled on somebody's lap. It looked like an elegant and quiet world.

When I pushed open the restaurant's door, it felt as if I had cracked open a vacuum seal. I stepped into the lush dining room, pulled off my cover as if I had entered a church, and watched a gorgeous hostess with bare shoulders, a long skirt, and a tight smile approach me.

"A table for . . . for one?"

"Yes."

"Smoking or nonsmoking."

"Smoking."

"Right this way." She escorted me to a table near the center of the room and waited for my approval.

It took a moment for me to realize what she was doing. "Fine."

She cleared away two of the place settings. It gave the impression that I was expecting someone.

I placed my cover on one of the empty seats and sat down.

"Shall I get you something from the bar?" She handed me a menu.

"Ahh. Yes. Scotch on the rocks."

She nodded and left my table without asking me for identification.

A waitress with a pitcher of ice water approached me from behind before I had a chance to open the menu. "Hello, I'm Robin."

"Hello, Robin."

"I'll be your waitress today." She picked up my empty glass and filled it with water. "Would you care for an appetizer?" She had brown eyes.

"I . . . I don't know. I haven't had time to look at the menu yet."

She set the water glass on the table. "Oh. Take your time."

"Thanks."

"Everything on the menu is good. I'll be back in a minute."

I opened the menu, but watched her walk away instead.

Cute figure. Pretty face.

I lit a cigarette and relaxed.

The beautiful hostess approached me as I lifted my napkin off the table, shook it free of its form, and draped it across my lap. She placed the drink in front of me.

"Thank you." I cradled my lit cigarette on the clean ashtray. "Do you know what time it is?"

"Sure." She glanced at her small wristwatch. "It's 2:35."

I pulled back my cuff and glanced at my wristwatch. "That's what mine says."

She was not amused. "Your waitress will be back in a moment."

"I don't need her as long as I have you." Her silence left me feeling awkward and stupid. "Sorry. That didn't come out right."

"You're out of practice."

"Actually, I've never been in practice. Sorry. I was behaving like an ordinary ex-serviceman."

"That looks like a uniform to me," she said.

"And it's on for the last time." I picked up my Scotch and took a drink. "This uniform represents what's left of my past, reveals what people think is my present, and now it's preventing me from stepping toward . . . toward the future."

"That sounds like you have a personal problem."

Her indifferent remark startled me. "I'll have another Scotch, please."

"I'll inform your waitress."

I set the glass on the table. "Thank you." I grabbed the smoldering cigarette from my ashtray, took a deep drag, and crushed it out. Then I opened the menu and hid behind it for what seemed to be a long time.

I stirred. I finished my drink.

Robin, my pixie waitress, finally approached me with a fresh drink and a smile. "Are you ready to order?"

"Sure." I made a random choice. I pointed at one of the entrees.

She placed my fresh drink on the table, peered over my shoulder at the menu, and read aloud as she scribbled down the order. "Fettucini Alfredo with chicken and smoked surrey sausage." She hit her order pad with the tip of her ballpoint

pen to emphasize that she had the order. "Will there be anything else?"

I shook my head and handed her the menu without making eye contact. I no longer felt present. She picked up my old
drink and left my table. I lit another cigarette and stared at
the amber liquid of the Scotch.

As my thoughts began to wander, I searched the past for
a memory that was something other than the war. Anything.
Anything:

"Doc."

"What?"

"Doc."

"What!"

"Are you awake?"

"What the—is that you, Gary?"

"Shhh. You want a beer?"

"I've had a beer."

"Got some downers, too."

"Now you're talking." I sat up on my rack and
reached for the beer. "It's warm."

"Check into the Waldorf Astoria if you want
good room service."

"Wise ass. Got a church key?"

"Here."

Foam bubbled out of the triangular opening on top of the beer can as soon as I used the
opener. "Shit."

"You're getting T.J.'s rack wet."

"Fuck him. He's passed out on mine."

"Thought so. Smells like puke over there."

"Crap. Let's get high." I dressed in my two-day-old, olive-green utilities that were draped over the foot of my rack. Then I pulled on my boots and screwed on my cover. "What time is it?"

"Does it matter? Do you have a hot date or something?"

"Smart ass."

"This is a.m. Sunday night, man."

I chugged down half the can of beer. "What the hell are waiting for?" They followed me out of the barracks, unto the second deck landing of the building, and into the moonlight. "Guantanamo fuckin' Bay, Cuba. Hell's bells. If this ain't the end of the world then I can see it."

"Yeah."

"Where are those downers?"

Gary reached into his right trouser pocket and fished them out. He presented nine capsules.

We chugged down three apiece with beer.

"Okay," I said. "Okay. This is good."

"There's a late movie showing," Gary said. "Come on."

We descended the stairs and zigzagged into the darkness toward an outdoor movie screen with a section of bleachers set in front of it.

"Got a cigarette?"

"Fuckin A."

As soon as we sat down to watch the movie, *Chitty Chitty Bang Bang*, it began to rain. But it didn't matter. This was Gitmo, Cuba, and we were in the U.S. Marine Corps and there were no women and there was no place else to go. So,

we cupped our cigarettes and pulled the brims of
our covers closer to our eyes and ignored the rain.
We gazed at the moving colors on the big screen
and listened to the Hollywood musical. We forgot our reason and paid no attention to the why
of our existence in our olive-green lives at the
end of the world.

The glass of amber liquid came into focus again.

I reached for the Scotch and took a drink.

I was stunned by the fact that my thoughts only went
back as far as my last duty station just before the war. What
had happened to my other life? Where was it?

I stood up. Robin was standing beside me with a tray.

She was frightened. "Is there anything wrong?"

"Wrong? No." I crushed out my cigarette and sat back
down. "I'm sorry."

"Here you are." She placed a plate of food in front of me
along with a small basket of bread. "Will there be anything else?"

"How about a bottle of beer."

"We have Miller, Schlitz, Bud—"

"Any kind. It doesn't matter."

"I'll be right back."

I picked up my fork and ate without interest. I smiled
when Robin returned with my beer. Our exchange was brief
and silent and formal.

I refueled myself with Fettucini and chicken before
drinking my beer and finishing my Scotch.

I had a sudden urge to scream, but I repressed it. My
hands gripped the edge of the table. I didn't understand this.

I stood up, reached for my wallet, and pulled out a twenty-
dollar bill. My hands were trembling. I laid the twenty-dollar

bill on the table and picked up the cloth napkin from the floor. I gazed at it as if it was something foreign then I wiped the sweat off my forehead.

I tossed the napkin on the table.

I was one week away from the bush. One week was all it took to process me out of the Navy and launch me into a civilian world that did not have a clue what the war was about.

I snatched my cover off the nearby chair and walked out of the restaurant into the busy airport terminal. I put on my cover then wandered about like a demented child. I didn't want to think, but I thought. And I remembered:

> Who the hell told John that he could die?
>
> They were waiting for us. We were traveling up the side of a hill and they were waiting for us.
>
> I felt a warm splatter on my face as I heard the sound of enemy contact: bits and pieces of small arms fire. I glanced to my right. Part of John's face was missing. I caught movement from the corner of my left eye, turned, and peered upward.
>
> Two VC. I blew away the first one with a single shot; the second one took three shots. I killed both of them.

The collision along the corridor didn't feel like an accident.

"Watch where you're going, you fascist pig," someone said.

I blinked at the guy in response.

He was tall and thin, pale and arrogant. His light brown hair hung to his shoulders and his eyes were covered by a pair of rose-colored sunglasses. He wore a jean jacket without a shirt underneath and a pair of tattered bell-bottom jeans that covered the tops of his dirty sandals. He had a canvas backpack slung over his right shoulder. "Why don't you watch where you're going?"

"Sorry."

"Typical. Well, sorry isn't enough. All you guys are just like."

"What guys?"

"You imperialist mother fuckers!"

I didn't understand this guy's hatred for me and I didn't like his tone. "I'll give you a motherfucker if you want one, Pal." As I took a threatening step toward him, I noticed a peace sign on a silver chain and several strands of beads hanging from his neck.

I checked my anger, raised my hand, and presented the universal peace sign with the middle and forefinger of my right hand in an effort to make contact with a living symbol of brotherhood that I had identified with in Vietnam via old magazines and newspapers from the world. "Peace, man."

The guy slapped off my cover. "You creep. You...you killer."

"What did you say to me, you son of a bitch?" I shoved the guy.

He shoved back.

I punched his left ear with my right fist. He leaned away from me holding his injured ear with both hands. I continued my assault with several jabs to his exposed right side. His cried out in pain. Then I grabbed him by the neck with both hands and choked him into a tangle of hair, beads, and chain.

Suddenly, I felt two sets powerful hands grab me by my upper arms. I was pulled away from him.

I glanced to my right and discovered police presence. I nodded. I grew calm. They released me.

"What's going on here?" one of the officers demanded.

"That creep." The hippie gasped. "He...he tried to kill me!" He massaged his throat. "Charges. I want to...to press charges."

"He started it, sir." I picked up my cover and put it on. "I was minding my own business when this jerk came along looking for trouble."

"Fascist pig!"

"Shut up!" the other officer warned.

"I'm pressing charges."

"Fine." The other officer took the guy by the upper arm. "Then come with me."

The guy pulled his arm away from the officer. "I'm not going anywhere with a cop."

"You said you wanted to press charges."

"Arrest him." He picked up his sunglasses and put them on. "That's what I want. You don't need me for that." Then he picked up his backpack and slung it over his right shoulder. "Pigs."

"Get out of here before I arrest you."

The guy turned his back to us and walked away as if he were immune to authority. The officers shook their heads.

"Are you alright?" one of the officers asked.

"Yes sir," I answered.

"We want you to come with us."

"I didn't do anything."

"I know. But we'd like to take you downstairs anyway."

"But—"

"Trust me." He glanced at his partner. "Trust us."

"Did you just get back?" the other officer asked.

"Yeah."

"Where were you?"

"Up North. I Corps. The DMZ."

"What outfit."

"First Recon. First Marine Division."

"We're ex-Marine Corps ourselves." The officer noted the caduceus above my third-class stripe. "Come with us, Doc."

A windowless corridor led to a windowless security office. There was a lady and two other guys in uniform sitting behind desks and not pretending to be busy.

"What have we got here?" the lady asked.

"Nothing" said one of the officers. He glanced at me. "Would you like a cup of coffee?"

"Sure."

The other officer pointed at a chair. "Have a seat."

I took off my cover and placed it on the nearby desktop before I sat down. "Thanks."

"You must be wondering why we're going through all this trouble."

"Yeah. I guess so. The other guy started the fight."

"That other guy doesn't count. You do." The officer dragged a chair away from a nearby desk, brought it close to me, and sat down. His partner presented me with a cup of black coffee.

I took a sip of the coffee. "So . . . so the fight—"

"Forget the fight. That's not it, Doc. You see, we've already received concerned phone calls from a bartender and a hostess."

I began to protest, but the officer raised his right forefinger to indicate that I should keep quiet.

"No." The officer shook his head for emphasis. "I said concerned. That means you weren't doing anything wrong. They were worried about your behavior. They are on your side."

"I see."

The officer who had given me the coffee scratched his head. "When did your flight get in?"

"This morning." I drank some of my coffee, set the cup on the desk near my cover, and lit a cigarette.

"Then why aren't you home?"

"Yeah. Haven't you been away long enough?"

I didn't answer them.

They exchanged glances.

"Isn't that a Purple Heart on your chest?"

"Yeah."

"And isn't that a Bronze Star?"

"Yeah."

"And that "V" stands for Valor, right?"

"Yeah."

The officer sitting next to me leaned against the back of his chair. "You're going to be alright."

The other officer approached a telephone and picked up the receiver. "Where do your parents live?"

"In Southwest Miami."

"What's their number."

"666-9875."

"You're going home," he said "Do you understand?"

I nodded.

I listened to the officer speak to my mother first, then to my father. He was very polite to them. He peered at me after he hung up the telephone. "You're father will be here shortly."

"Thank you."

They let me drink coffee and smoke cigarettes in silence while I waited for my father.

My father arrived in a blink of an eye. I did not get up from my chair when I saw him enter the airport's security office.

My father was a short powerful man who walked with a strong steady gait and who saw the world through a pair of

serious gray eyes, which lightened immediately when he saw
me stand up.

"Hello, Pop."

"Son."

We embraced each other. And when I felt his kiss against
my right cheek, I returned the kiss.

My father was on the verge of tears. "Have you eaten?"

I nodded. "How's Mom?"

"She's waiting for us at the house." My father addressed
one of the officers. "What is my . . . ." He peered at me. "What
are you doing here?" He addressed the officer again. "Is he
free to go home?"

"Yes sir, of course," the officer answered.

I wanted to express my gratitude to the officers, but I
couldn't.

One of the officers handed me my cover. "Welcome home."

"Thanks." Then I left the security office with my father.

"Are you alright?" my father asked.

"Sure, Pop. Do you mind if we stop and get my seabag?"

"Of course not."

A comfortable silence accompanied us as we walked to
the airport locker where I had stowed my seabag. Once there,
my father took my cover from my hand.

I noted my father's increased baldness as I reached into
my pocket for the key.

"You look mighty good, Son."

"So do you, Pop." I inserted the key into the lock. The scent
of canvas assaulted me as soon as I opened the door. I leaned
against the edge of the dark square opening. I felt my father's
tender hand on my shoulder. "It's good to be back, Pop."

"I know."

"Who the hell am I now?"

"I thought the same thing when I got back from the war in Okinawa."

"You too?"

"Of course, Son. War. It's always the same."

"Why didn't you tell me?"

"Go ahead. Tell somebody who's never been there. Go ahead." My Father shook his head. "Words. You'll see. And . . . and the war is never over."

"Your . . . your World War II—"

"Happened yesterday. And that's okay." My Father hugged me then maneuvered me away from the locker and pulled out my seabag.

"I'll get that, Pop."

My father placed my cover on my head. "No way. I'm the one taking you home."

I did not resist his protectiveness.

With sympathy, I listened to my father's labored breathing caused by the burden of the seabag. It was a labor of love. Love. But I was glad when we finally reached the car.

My father dropped the seabag on the parking lot's pavement and allowed me to toss it into the trunk when he opened it. Then he offered me the car keys. "Do you want to drive?" he wheezed.

This was my father's supreme compliment.

"No. Take us home."

The car keys disappeared into my father's fist; it was a gesture that revealed his pleasure in maintaining possession of them. "Come on. Your mother's probably standing by the front door."

"Probably." I stepped into the front passenger side of the car and sat down. "She'll probably have coffee made."

My father started the car. "Probably." He eased the car out of the parking lot.

The Miami sky was big and blue and clear.

I relaxed and listened to my father talk about the bad traffic. I closed my eyes and suddenly realized that I was looking forward to feeling my mother's embrace.

GLOSSARY

AK-47 The basic infantry weapon used by the NVA and the VC

ARVN Army of the Republic of Vietnam

AO Area of Operation; Action Officer

The World Home; America

Billet A personnel position or assignment filled by one person

black wall The Vietnam War Memorial

bush Vietnam jungle/battleground

C-4 Plastic, putty textured, explosive that burns like sterno when lit and used to heat C-rations and water

CH-46 Sea Knight; a twin-rotor helicopter used to transport troops and cargo

Caca dau Vietnamese phrase for "I'll kill you."

Charlie A member of the Viet Cong; or the Viet Cong collectively

Chicom Chinese Communist or weapons manufactured in China Chieu hoi. "Open arms." A program under which amnesty was offered to VC defectors

Chieu hoi "Open arms." A program under which amnesty was offered to VC defectors.

chow hall Dining hall

church key Beer can opener

clap Gonorrhea

claymore mine A type of antipersonnel land mine

click Kilometer

cover Hat

C-rations (C-rats) Prepared food in cans, provided to troops where fresh food is unavailable or cooking is impossible

chopper Helicopters

Da Nang A major Northern city in Vietnam

Deck Floor

ditty bag Small travel bag used to store a man's toiletry

dinky dow Vietnamese term (dinky dau) for "Crazy" or "You're crazy."

Dive Locker The name, and the location, of First Recon's small unit of Combat divers

DMZ Demilitarized Zone

D-ring D-shaped metal link used to hold gear together

Dung lai Vietnamese phrase for "Stop" or "Halt."

EM Club Enlisted bar

entrenching tool A small folding shovel

Fifty Cal. .50-caliber machine gun

FMF Fleet Marine Force

Fragged To deliberately kill an unpopular senior officer (usually with a grenade)

frag Grenade

fragged for a patrol Assigned to a patrol

friendly fire Weapons fire coming from one's own side, especially fire that causes accidental injury or death to one's own forces

Gitmo, Cuba Guantanamo Bay, Cuba (originally: GTMO, Cuba)

Grunt Marine infantryman; also a general term used for any combatant in a special forces unit like First Recon

gunships Huey and Cobra Helicopters

HE High explosives

Heads Guys who smoke marijuana

hooches Roughly constructed building used for living quarters

I Corps One of four corps of the Army of the Republic of Vietnam; the Northern most region of South Vietnam bordering North Vietnam where the U.S. Marine Corps had a large presence

in-country Vietnam

I.V. Intravenous

Jarhead. A marine

Juicers. Guys who drank alcohol

Joint Marijuana

K-bar Combat knife

KIA Killed in action

Liberty Shore leave

long-rations (long-rats) Dehydrated food in hermetically sealed bags

LZ Landing Zone

Magazine A chamber for holding a supply of cartridges to be fed automatically to the breech of a gun

medevac Medical evacuation, usually by helicopter

MPC Military Payment Certificate

M-14 An American Military selective fire automatic rifle

M-16 An American Military semi automatic and automatic rifle

M-79 Grenade launcher

NCO Non-commissioned Officer

NVA North Vietnamese Army

office-pogue A pejorative for non combatant office clerk

OP Observation post

Pogue A pejorative for rear echelon support personnel, a Marine not of the combat arms

pogey-bait Candy or sweets

PRC-25 Portable field radio carried by the RTO (also known as: Prick 25)

P-38 Military can opener for C-rats

Rate Navy enlisted term for rank. Naval Officers have rank, enlisted personnel have *rates* and *ratings*. A rating is a name given to an occupation such as a *corpsman*. A rate is a paygrade (Petty Officer Third Class—PO3), which is combined with a rating (Hospital Corpsman Third Class—HM3). Hence, when asked, the rate is third class, the rating is corpsman.

Rack Cot/bed

Recon Reconnaissance; also an elite fighting force in the Marine Corps

R & R Rest and Recreation (Recuperation)

RPG Rocket-propelled grenade

RTO Radio telephone operator who carried the PRC-25

saddle up Put on one's backpack and get ready to go

seabag A canvas duffel bag used to carry one's personal belongings

skivvies Underwear

SKS A semi-automatic carbine used by the NVA and the VC

squid/squidly A pejorative for sailor

S-2 Intelligence

tail-end-charlie The Marine who guards the rear of a recon team

VC Viet Cong

web belt Canvas belt

web belt harness A web belt with suspenders to support the weight of ammo pouches, grenades, and canteens that are attached to the belt

web gear Canvas belt and shoulder straps (suspenders) used for packing equipment and ammunition for patrols (782 gear)

white hat Sailor's hat; another name for sailor

WP White Phosphorous Grenade; Willy Peter

WIA Wounded in action

Z-boat A black inflatable boat with an outboard motor

782 gear Standard issue web gear (combat gear) including: web belt, suspenders, harness, backpack, ammo pouches, canteens, and canteen pouches, etc.

AUTHOR'S BIOGRAPHY

D.S. Lliteras is the author of twelve books that have received national and international acclaim. Some of his novels have been translated into Italian, Russian, and Japanese. His short stories and poetry have appeared in numerous national and international magazines, journals, and anthologies.

D.S. Lliteras enlisted in the U.S. Navy after high school and served in Vietnam as a combat corpsman attached to the First Reconnaissance Battalion, First Marine Division, earning a Bronze Star Medal (with Combat "V") for valor. While in country, Lliteras completed twenty long-range reconnaissance patrols and eighty combat dives.

After his discharge in 1970, he enrolled at Florida State University where he received his Bachelor of Arts and Master of Fine Arts degrees.

Lliteras worked as a theatrical director until 1979 then quit directing and became a merchant sailor. In 1981, he earned a commission in the U.S. Navy and served as a Deep Sea Diving and Salvage Officer. After several years of service, which included extreme, arduous sea duty, Lliteras resigned his naval commission and became a professional fire fighter.

After retiring from the fire department, he has been able to devote his full time to writing fiction.

His Wikipedia address is *http://en.wikipedia.org/wiki/D._S._ Lliteras.*

Endorsements for *Flames and Smoke Visible*

"Every now and then a clear voice rises from the ashes of America's fireground and Dan Lliteras is one of these. A former fire fighter, Lliteras knows the voice of urgency and crisis, elements that make you feel you are there with the characters in his stories. He is a writer to watch, and to read."

—Dennis Smith, author of *Report from Engine Co. 82*

"I read *Flames and Smoke Visible* non-stop, in a space of a few hours—I was totally caught up in the drama of fire fighting. With the authority of experience as a fire fighter, and the talent and the skill honed as the author of many brilliant novels, Mr. Lliteras has produced a beautifully written, riveting account about this profession that is not only a first-rate entertaining book but also a book which informs, instructs, and allows the reader access to the human heart."

—David Willson, author of *REMF Diary: A Novel of the Vietnam War Zone* and editor of *Vietnam War Generation Journal*

"In heartfelt, unadorned prose, Lliteras, a fiction writer, fire fighter, and Vietnam veteran, writes of his experience as a uniformed member of a fire department in Norfolk, Virginia. He writes of the hazards, challenges, and camaraderie of the job. Lliteras has been at war on two fronts, fighting both enemy soldiers and raging fires, and there is a hard-earned wisdom in these true-life episodes that grips our attention."

—*Publishers Weekly*

"If you're looking for a tiny window into the life of a firefighter, look no further than novelist and former fireman Lliteras's latest book. A decent, quick read . . . this brief glimpse into both the mundane and exciting moments in a firefighter's career is sobering. Recommended."

—*Library Journal*

Rainbow Ridge Books publishes spiritual, metaphysical, and self-help titles, and is distributed by Square One Publishers in Garden City Park, New York.

To contact authors and editors, peruse our titles, and see submission guidelines, please visit our website at
www.rainbowridgebooks.com.